Hungry

Hungry

A Novel By
A.L. Glennon

IngramElliott

Published by IngramElliott, Inc.
www.ingramelliott.com
9815-J Sam Furr Road, Suite 271, Huntersville NC 28078

This is a work of fiction. The names, characters, places, or events used in this book are the product of the author's imagination or used fictitiously. Any resemblance to actual people (alive or deceased) events, or locales is completely coincidental.

Book design by Maureen Cutajar, gopublished.com
Cover design by Jeanine Henning, jeaninehenning.com
Editing by F. Barnes

ISBN Hardcover: 978-1-952961-15-1
ISBN Paperback: 978-1-952961-16-8
ISBN E-Book: 978-1-952961-17-5

Library of Congress Control Number: 2023939242

Subjects: Fiction—General. Fiction—Coming of Age. Fiction—Family Life/General. Fiction—Dance, Theater & Musicals. Fiction—Romance/New Adult.

Published in the United States of America.
Printed in the United States of America.
First Edition: 2023, First International Edition: 2023

To Sebastian, Reese, and Caden.
I love you.

Acknowledgments

Thank you to everyone who has encouraged me throughout my writing journey! I am especially grateful to Sebastian, Reese, and Caden for believing in me, telling me to stick with it, and inspiring me every day. I love you.

I'm grateful to the IngramElliott team for welcoming me and my novel so enthusiastically and for making the path to publication as smooth as possible.

Thank you to Darcey—the Wordsmiths are a huge reason I still write, and I am grateful for all of your advice. Geoff, thank you for always being brutally honest in the best possible way. I am grateful for your critiques and your friendship.

Thank you, reader, for choosing to spend your time with Sulie, Cam, and Serge. It is an honor to share their story with you.

Chapter One

"I can't believe you did this, Sulie."

My mom almost never curses, but she can make my name sound like a four-letter word when she wants to.

"Honestly. First, you show up wearing *that*..." She gestures toward the best part of my outfit. "And then you go out of your way to make your grandmother look like a Las Vegas show girl. I really don't know what's the matter with you."

I feel sorry for my mother sometimes. She's a control freak who got stuck with art-prone me and spontaneous Grandma Nell, two quirky souls far beyond her control who have never once, in my mother's opinion, done anything right. Not even dying, which my Grandma Nell just did two days ago.

My mother was super pissed that Grandma kicked it on Wednesday because Mom was supposed to host her single-mom support group at our house that night, and she'd had to cancel. I agree that it was inconvenient. Clearly, my mother could really use some support right now. She's alternating between taking jabs at me and my dead grandmother and sobbing into a fistful of Kleenex.

"I hope you're happy," she says to me through a fresh round of tears. I roll my eyes because, really, how big of an asshole would I have to be to admit that I'm happy at a funeral? "You and your grandmother both look ridiculous."

I look down at the rainbow poncho I've thrown on over the funeral garb my mother bought for me: a black knee-length sheath dress, black stockings, and black shoes my mother keeps referring to as "pumps." With my dark hair and eyes and my wraith-pale skin, the outfit makes me look like a corpse myself. The many-hued poncho really gives my whole look a much-needed pop of color, I think. Colors, plural, I guess. Bright, eye-straining, unadulterated colors. Grandma Nell crocheted the poncho by hand from some of the softest yarn I've ever felt. It's comforting and warm, and it still smells vaguely like Grandma. Wearing the poncho is like wearing one of her hugs. This poncho wrapped around me is the only thing holding me together right now. If I took it off for even a second, my tightly wound chest would explode. The yarn poncho is as much a piece of survival gear as it is a fashion statement.

As for Grandma Nell, she looks beautiful. She would have hated the crappy gray pantsuit my mother had the funeral director put her in for the occasion. I had no choice but to accessorize it a little bit with a silver sequined headband, a peacock brooch set with purple and blue crystals, a bright-blue crocheted scarf, and an oversized cuff bracelet. I snuck into the funeral parlor a few minutes before the rest of the mourners arrived to make sure Grandma was presentable. It was the least I could do for her. My mother should be thanking me instead of lashing out.

My Aunt Alice arrives in a miasma of expensive perfume and cigarette smoke.

2

"Laurel?" she says to my mother after she's kissed us both on the cheek. "How are you holding up?"

She hugs my mother, and I'm grateful to have her distracted. Aunt Alice is my father's sister, and, even though he's been out of the picture since I was an infant, she and my mother have kept in touch a little bit.

My mother sobs into the shoulder of Alice's coat.

"Maybe you need to get some air," Alice says to my mother. "Huh? Let's step outside." Alice looks kind of on edge, tugging at a strand of pearls around her neck. I bet she hates funerals, that the idea of death makes her wildly uncomfortable. I think she just wants to step outside and smoke, but my mother nods and lets herself be led away. "We'll be right back, Sulie, OK?" Alice says to me over her shoulder, but she doesn't wait for me to tell her whether or not it's OK to maroon me here in front of Grandma Nell's open casket.

Before I have time to feel super lonely or awkward or think about how I'd much rather be at home alone with my sketchbook, Cam plops down into my mother's recently vacated front-row seat like he's been eyeing it for a while, waiting for his chance to pounce. Which he probably has. "I love this," he says, fiddling with the edge of my rainbow poncho and smiling. "It's so Grandma Nell. And it looks great on you."

Cam is my best friend. Technically, he's pretty much my only friend. He's known Grandma Nell almost as long as I have.

"My mom is pissed," I say.

Cam shrugs. "Are you OK?" he asks me. "Holding up all right and everything?"

"Yeah."

Cam fidgets. He's not comfortable sitting still. "This is a great funeral, huh?" he says.

I give him a look.

"I mean, a good turnout or whatever." He glances around the room a little awkwardly, and I follow his gaze. It's getting pretty crowded, and the actual service isn't even supposed to start for another twenty minutes. "Those Senior Stars ladies are really cool." He nods toward the back of the room where a group of older women is decked out in colorful blouses and big jewelry that my mother probably finds indecorous. They're talking loudly and laughing like they're here for cocktail hour instead of to say goodbye forever to one of their most beloved members. "They have tons of great stories about your grandma." Cam is smiling at me. "They've been talking my ear off."

I try to smile back. "That's great," I say.

The Senior Stars is a social club my grandma belonged to. More than belonged to. Lived for. I'm glad they've taken Cam under their wing for the afternoon so I don't have to worry about him feeling out of place while his parents voluntarily man the guest book and pass out funeral programs. Not that I ever have to worry about always-has-his-shit-together Cam.

Cam and I sit in comfortable silence until Aunt Alice leads my sniffling mother back into the room and the funeral director indicates he'd like to get this show on the road by standing up front, clearing his throat, and looking at his watch a lot. Cam gives my shoulder a comforting little squeeze before relinquishing my mother's seat to her.

The funeral service would only seem weird to anyone who didn't know Grandma Nell which, one would hope, everyone at her funeral did. My mother sits on the edge of her seat next to me as it starts, and I can feel her tense up even more as it gets underway, hating each minute of the proceedings more than the last. She fidgets, crossing and uncrossing her legs. She sighs repeatedly, her annoyance coming off her in waves that, thankfully, my soft, crocheted poncho absorbs before they can affect me. Because I love the service. I think it's perfect.

Grandma preplanned and prepaid for her own funeral, and, even though my mother tried, she was not allowed to alter the program. First, an old friend of Grandma Nell's named Gordo stands up and plays John Lennon's "Woman" on the saxophone with some cheesy recorded background music to accompany him. His off-white suit should look out of place among all the dark-clad mourners, but I think Grandma Nell would have liked it. His dark skin shines with a thin sheen of sweat as he plays, eyes closed, swaying back and forth to the music, completely lost in the song. When he's done, he swipes at his face with a silky-looking bright-blue handkerchief he pulls from his breast pocket. Then, with both laughter and tears, he tells us that Grandma Nell was probably the love of his life and he remembers dancing with her in an overheated school gym at some kind of formal event a million years ago.

Next, one of the Senior Stars ladies limps to the stage with the aid of a large cane, costume jewelry jangling, curly bright-white hair springing in every direction. She licks her dark-red-lipstick-covered lips and then reads a baddish poem she wrote about my grandma called "Walking Loudly." The gist of it seems to be that Grandma Nell was such a presence that you could hear and feel her coming from a mile away. "She stomps the solid earth/Gentle giantess in spritely form/Newborn old-soul spirit/Tremors announce her coming…"

Another elderly Stars gal in a black leotard and a long, flowy skirt adorned with jingly gold coins performs an elaborate belly dance that she says is in Grandma's honor. She tells us all that they took lessons together on one of their Senior Stars trips. Everyone but my mother experiences violent paroxysms of laughter as my grandmother's friend rolls her way-over-the-hill hips in time to some intense, Middle Eastern–sounding music. I swear, even the dancer herself isn't able to keep a straight face.

I know Grandma Nell put her friend up to this just to needle my mom. And it's working beautifully. It's an amazing performance, some of the best live entertainment I've ever seen. When she finally finishes to thunderous applause and wolf whistles from the rowdy Senior Stars crowd, I turn around to catch Cam's eye. He's sitting with the other Stars, whooping it up and wiping away tears with funeral-home tissues. There's not a dry eye in the place in the best possible way. My grandmother would have loved it.

Eventually, some officiant gets up and says a bunch of stuff about God and loss and reads a eulogy that Grandma wrote herself. It's one sentence: "She loved her life and all the people in it." Hearing that makes some of Grandma's loved ones tear up in a sad way again.

But nobody's sad for long because while Grandma's hearse heads for the crematorium (which she insisted all her mourners skip), the rest of us are headed to a repast at Tony Baloney's Deli, the Senior Stars' favorite place to eat. It's exactly what it sounds like, a hole-in-the-wall deli, but their hot pastrami sandwiches are to die for. Or, at least, they're definitely the perfect comfort food to eat after someone else dies.

The drive to Tony's is tense. My mother taps the steering wheel with her thumbs. I distract myself by remembering the belly dancer shaking what's left of what God gave her right up there next to Grandma Nell's casket, and I start to laugh. My mother looks like she could spit nails at me, so I pull my poncho tighter around myself and pretend that I'm sobbing. Then, my mom relaxes a little. I can tell it's been bothering her that I haven't shed a tear for my beloved grandmother yet. I guess she figures fake tears are better than nothing.

Tony's isn't really big enough to handle Grandma Nell's whole crowd, but nobody seems to care. When there aren't any more chairs, people stand. When the inside of the deli gets too crowded, people hang around out front on the sidewalk. Everyone is animated and joking and talking about the belly dancer, calling for an encore she waves off graciously but firmly. Only my mom is straight-faced, looking down her nose at the inside of Tony Baloney's with its chipped-laminate tabletops, discolored posters of famous Italian landmarks, and baseboards thick with decades of grease and grime.

Tony (whose real last name is Bonetti, not Baloney) is loving the whole thing, of course. It's probably the most business he's ever had in a single day, and he and his one other staff member are making their way through the crowd carrying trays piled high with my grandma's favorite sandwiches and offering chips and pickles and cans of soda to all the happy mourners.

Cam's parents and Aunt Alice sit front-and-center with my mom, consoling her or whatever, but Cam and I sit with a few Senior Stars in the back of the room. These ladies are sad too, but they need no consolation. Grandma's friend, May, has a flask in her purse, and she's spiking her friends' Diet Cokes. She holds the flask out to me and Cam with a question on her face, and Cam waves her off, but I give her a go-ahead nod. She tips the flask up, and some clear liquid dribbles into my soda can. I pick it up and take a sip, curious. The number of parties I've been to in my eighteen years on earth is pitiful, and I don't drink much. The soda tastes different now, less sweet. I think I like it. I know it's physically impossible, but I immediately feel drunk.

"Tell her the one about the Nashville trip," Cam says to May and her friends. "Sulie, you've got to hear this!"

May laughs, which sets the chandelier earrings she's worn for the occasion swinging. The lady to her right, Theresa, says, "Oh, let me, let me! So, OK. The time we went to Nashville? Right after the bus pulls in, we drop our stuff at the hotel and go out to do some sightseeing. We took that tour...what was that tour called?"

"Talking Trash," May says, shrugging out of her funeral blazer and revealing a zebra-striped blouse underneath.

"No," another Senior Star, Addie, pipes up, reaching for May's flask with a hand encrusted in sparkly rings. "It was called Trashy Nashy."

"Smashed Nashville!" another eavesdropping Star shouts in passing.

"You were smashed in Nashville," Theresa mutters at her back. She rolls her heavily made-up eyes at us. "Well, anyway. So, we went on some kind of comedic sightseeing tour in a special tour bus and—"

"Remember that bus had no air conditioning?" May says.

"Remember the driver's hair?" Addie says, pouring generously from May's flask. "Sally said it was a wig, but I said it wasn't, remember? And then Geraldine tried to settle the whole thing by attempting to pull it off, and it turned out, yup, it was her real hair all right. Really curly, but all natural. Just wild!"

"So, anyway…" Theresa gives Addie a stop-talking-about-the-hair look. "We take this sightseeing bus on the tour, and it drops us at a restaurant where we had a reservation for dinner, and our charter bus is supposed to pick us up there afterward and take us back to the hotel. So, after dinner, we go out front, and there's a bus, just waiting there at the curb. Nell pushes open the door and gets on…and then she comes running back off, screaming and laughing and talking gibberish."

The other ladies are laughing at the memory of my grandmother freaking out on a Nashville sidewalk.

"It wasn't our charter bus after all," Theresa continues, "but a tour bus for some hot new country-western band that was supposed to be playing at the bar next to the restaurant, and your grandmother got on board just as the fine-looking young singer was changing his pants, and she saw him in the altogether!"

"Isn't that crazy?" Cam asks me. He's grinning from ear to ear even though he's already heard this story.

"Nuts," I say, pulling my poncho around me and taking a long swig of my Coke-and-Whatever-May-Is-Serving.

"But that's not all," Addie says, her many rings clinking as she claps her hands in delight. "The young man was so upset about having offended your grandmother—even though the whole thing was her own blessed fault—that he invited us all to his show that night, and we got to sit right in the front, in the *VIP* section, and he even dedicated a song to Nell called, 'Hot Lovin' Mama!' It was hysterical!"

I try to laugh along with Grandma's friends, and I wonder for the millionth time what it would be like to be Grandma Nell, to be someone who gets invited on trips with big groups of friends, to be someone people tell funny stories about and play love songs on the saxophone for and humor with a belly dance, to be someone nobody will ever forget.

Eventually, one by one, Grandma's myriad, zany loved ones take their leave. They all hug me goodbye and compliment me on my rainbow poncho and ask me to stay in touch. The saxophone player strokes my hair and tells me I look just like Nellie when she was young, and the belly dancer tells me I have my grandmother's spark, whatever that is. She's thrown a leopard-print jacket on over her leotard for the repast, but she's still wearing the jingly skirt, and she clinks pleasantly as she heads out the door. Aunt Alice says she has to get going as well. Something about Uncle Jim and cousin Henry expecting her at a very important sportsball playoff game she just can't miss. She's sure we understand.

When everyone is finally gone and Cam's parents have frowned at him knowingly and asked him repeatedly whether he was fit to drive his car home before deciding to take off themselves, Cam and I wait on the sidewalk while my mother talks to Tony.

"Thanks for being here," I say. "You didn't have to come."

"Yes, I did. Are you kidding me? I'm really going to miss Grandma Nell. I'm so sorry, Sulie. Really."

Cam sounds like he might cry. I really wish he wouldn't. I'm absolute shit at comforting people. A little, "There, there…" and a pat on the shoulder is usually the best I can do.

"She really liked you," I tell Cam, because it's true, and it will mean a lot to him to hear it.

Cam does perk up a little. "Remember when she used to bake those little cakes—her Sunday cakes, she called them—and we'd hide out under the kitchen table and she'd pretend she didn't see us reaching up and stealing them?" Obviously, Cam hasn't tired of Grandma Nell stories just yet. "She'd be all like, 'Oh, heavens me! I'd have sworn there were four more cakes here a minute ago! Oh well, better make another batch.'" Cam actually does a great impression of my grandmother.

"Yeah," I say. "I remember."

"Camden?" My mother appears beside us, carrying a big white take-out bag with what must be a ton of leftover pastrami sandwiches in it. "Do you need a ride, honey?" My mother looks like too much of a wreck to safely drive the two of us, let alone a neighbor kid, home, but she asks anyway.

"No, thanks," Cam says. "I have my car." He gives my mom an awkward hug, careful not to squash the big bag of sandwiches she holds in front of her like a shield. Cam lets go of my mother and looks at me. "Call me," he says. "OK?"

I nod. We've never been super touchy-feely, me and Cam, so I offer him my fist to bump.

"Come on," he says. "It's a funeral! You're mourning! I'm comforting you, damn it, whether you like it or not." Cam throws his arms around me, and I can't breathe for a split second, and then I inhale way too deeply. Cam smells amazing, so clean, so Cam, so…alive. And I finally lose it, right there on the sidewalk in front of Tony Baloney's, and let out all the sobs that have been building up inside of me since Grandma Nell stopped living on Wednesday.

My mom wanted me to go to pieces, but she didn't necessarily want to deal with me going to pieces, so she's more than happy to let Cam drive me home. We sit in my driveway for a long time, long enough for me to wish the car were still running, the heat still flowing out of the vents in dry, comforting waves. I hug myself inside my crocheted poncho.

"What can I do?" Cam asks. "How can I make this better?"

I look at Cam's face, his familiar, safe, honest face. He's probably just average-looking with brown hair and brown eyes, but he has this smile that takes over his whole face—takes over everything within a one-mile radius, even—and makes him absolutely Prince-Charming gorgeous. Lucky for him (and most of womankind), Cam is pretty much always smiling. But he's not smiling now, of course, because I've been crying in his car all the way home, and I feel a huge wave of guilt about the concern on his suddenly plain, unhappy face. Cam is a person who always wants to fix everything. I'm a person who thinks it's OK for some things to be broken.

"There's nothing you can do," I tell him, "but thanks."

I go to get out of the car, opening the door so a wave of cold air passes right through my yarn poncho.

"What are you doing tomorrow?" Cam asks.

"I dunno," I say. "Catching up on schoolwork, maybe." This is a lie. I'm not making up anything I missed this week. My grandmother freaking died, OK? I think that should buy me a pass on an essay or two. At least.

"I'll come over," Cam says. He's grinning again. He figures his presence alone will be enough to cheer me up. He's probably right. "I should have the afternoon off tomorrow."

"OK," I say. "See ya."

I get out of the car before I can burst into tears again and hurry into the house. My mom is in the kitchen with a glass of wine. I guess May didn't hook her up from her flask at the no-liquor-license Tony Baloney's. Her shoulders slump, her hair hangs limply around her face, and her eye makeup is smudged. Her once-perfect funeral suit is wrinkled now, and she closes her eyes with exhaustion as she takes a long sip from her glass. I know I should stay up and talk with my mom, that her mother just died and, in her own way, she's as sad about it as I am. But I can't. There's something else I need to do, and it can't wait another minute.

"I'm tired," I say. "Goodnight."

"'Night," my mother replies into her wine glass.

I hurry down the hall to the bathroom and lock myself in. I pull my arms underneath my poncho, reach a hand inside the neckline of my little black funeral dress, and feel inside my bra. I grope around in there, starting to panic, and then I feel it, the thing that I've been thinking about almost nonstop since the funeral, and I relax. I grasp it and pull it out, a long, silver strand of hair. I'd managed to snag it from Grandma's head while I was arranging the sequined headband in her hair back at the funeral home. It's so long that I'd thought I could make it last for a while, stretch it out over the course of a few days or something, but it's been such a stressful, sad, god-awful day that I know this is a one-shot deal.

I coil the long hair into my mouth and swallow it.

Chapter Two

The day after Grandma's funeral, my mother tells me she supposes we have to deal with Grandma's things. She means get rid of all her stuff and make it like she never even lived here. Naturally, I balk. My mom insists, though, and leads me to Grandma's bedroom. I stop at the doorway, not wanting to cross the threshold. This is where Grandma died. It feels like hallowed ground. And maybe it's just a little bit creepy too.

My mother's already been in here, I can tell. Grandma's feather-trimmed purple bedside lampshades are gone, replaced with plain white ones, and her bulletin board full of postcards, photos, and mementos from her travels has been taken down, leaving a weird, dark-colored rectangle behind on the wall where it had hung. My mom has stripped the bed, too, cleaned the mattress, covered it back over with Grandma's purple flowered comforter, and put shams on the pillows to give the room the illusion of being lived in, but I can see a bare mattress corner peeking out near the head of the bed. The whole room looks like a lie.

"This would make a pretty guest room," my mom says. "Don't you think?"

I can't remember the last time we had a guest.

"Or maybe a nice art studio for you?" In a rare maternal gesture, my mother reaches up to brush a few strands of un-washed hair out of my eyes, and I flinch and pull away. A dark curtain of hair falls across my face, and I leave it there, an act of defiance even though it's really annoying to have a big chunk of hair in my eyes. At least it partially obscures my view of my mother going over to Grandma Nell's closet and frown-ing at the contents.

"OK," my mother says, "some of this is just junk." She pulls a furry robe out of the closet and tosses it on the floor.

I rush in to rescue it.

"This was her favorite robe!" I say.

"Well, it shows," my mother says. "Look at the thing. It's all matted, stained."

My mother's right, but I don't want to admit it.

"Honestly," my mother says, pulling an armload of brightly colored sweaters and wraps from the closet. "How much cro-chet could one person wear?"

My grandmother had taken up crocheting a number of years ago, and she was always wearing her colorful, interesting cre-ations. My mother dumps Grandma's handywork on the rug, and then reaches back in to pull out a huge bunch of oversized purses. Grandma loved those purses, carried a different one every day. Some of them she made herself out of quilt squares or yarn. Some she bought at thrift shops or discovered on shopping excursions with her friends. They were always full of makeup and scarves and jewelry and snacks and perfume samples and her favorite peppermints. They were always full of Grandma. My mom is just tossing them into a pile like they don't matter at all.

"Stop," I say. Something in my voice makes my mother look at me with sympathy.

"We can start smaller," she says, "if you want. Here." She pulls open a dresser drawer. "Socks and leg warmers," she says, shaking her head a little. "We can let those go, can't we?"

My grandmother was the only old lady I knew who could rock the leg-warmer look. So, no, in my opinion, those should stay too.

"And, obviously, this is all garbage," my mom says as she pulls open two drawers completely packed with tiny little hotel soaps, shampoos, and body lotions.

"It's not garbage," I say. "She got those on all her Senior Stars road trips."

"So?"

"So she liked them. They meant something to her. She said she thought it was neat how when you travel, you smell different because you leave your regular soap at home."

My mother just stares at me for a minute, then she sighs like I've completely worn her out. "Sulie," she says, "I don't know what you want me to do here. Your grandmother's gone. We can't just keep this room as a time capsule, a shrine."

I know this. Intellectually, I know this. I cross my arms and scowl in defiance anyway.

"Look," my mom says, "Why don't you take some time to go through her things yourself, pick out a few items you'd like to keep—things you can actually use, mind you—and then we'll donate the rest to the church ladies? OK?"

No, it's not OK. None of this is OK.

"OK, Sulie?"

"Whatever."

My mother sighs and leaves me standing there in the mess she made. I can't believe she doesn't want anything of her mother's. But then I try to picture my mom in one of Grandma's glittery brooches or wearing one of her bright, crocheted scarves, and I have to laugh just a little. Which makes me feel guilty. Which makes me want to cry.

I sink down into the pile of Grandma's worldly possessions, dig out a sparkly gold shawl, and wrap myself up in it. I sit cross-legged like some kind of gold-shawled fortune teller staring into the pile of Grandma's stuff as if it were a crystal ball with all of life's answers inside. And that's how Cam finds me when he comes over a couple hours later.

"Hey," he says, hovering in the doorway, bouncing on his toes a little. "Sorry I'm late. Rehearsal ran kind of long after all."

Cam's a dancer. A really good one. Ballet. He has two performances and an audition this month. He's been rehearsing his butt off. It's actually a miracle they let him out of the studio at a decent hour for a change, especially since he did the unthinkable and missed rehearsal yesterday to be at Grandma Nell's funeral.

"Um," Cam says, stepping into the room. "What's going on?" He looks around at the crochet and the purses and the drawers full of shampoo.

"My mom wants to get rid of Grandma," I tell him.

"Oh," he says. He comes and sits down next to me, careful not to step on any of Grandma's things. He picks up one of her handmade shawls and runs his fingers over it almost reverently.

"She's just going to give it all to the Women's Fellowship Thrift Shop at Our Lady of WhoGivesAShit."

"Huh." Cam cracks his neck.

"All this!" I tell him loudly because he doesn't seem to be getting upset enough. "The stuff that she loved! The handbags, the sweaters, the scarves! It's all going to a thrift shop so a bunch of lame-ass bargain hunters—maybe even some of Grandma's own friends—can paw through it all and judge every piece and say things like, 'What do you think of this?' and 'Yes! That's perfect for my Halloween costume!' and 'Oh, this one's awful,' and cast it all aside and—"

"Sulie?" Cam's doing that not-smiling thing again and fidgeting kind of nervously. "Just chill, OK?"

At the mention of the word chill, I feel cold. I grab a handmade scarf and knot it around my neck.

Cam runs a hand through his hair, messing it up in kind of a cool-looking way and sighs. He seems really tired. He's been tired a lot lately. All his extra rehearsals are killing him, and now I'm killing him too.

"What can I do to help?" he asks. "Want me to start sorting things into piles? Or emptying some of the drawers?"

"I don't know," I say.

"Do you want me to leave you alone?" he asks.

"No."

Cam picks up a gold lamé handbag big enough to hold a bowling ball and turns it over in his hands. He looks at the pile of stuff around us a little helplessly, then he jumps up, completely reenergized with a huge smile on his face.

"I have. The best. Idea!" he says. His eyes are sparkling like the glitziest of Grandma's rhinestone-encrusted handbags.

Chapter Three

Cam is too creative, too cool, too smoking hot, too awesome in general to be my friend. I know it. Everyone knows it. Everyone, apparently, except Cam. He and I have been best buds since we were toddlers in the neighborhood together. In fact, we were each other's only real friends throughout elementary and middle school, both artsy dorks relegated to the fringes of school society.

But then, overnight, Cam blossomed into a popular kid, with pretty girls lusting after him and cool jocks offering him fists to bump in the school hallways, while I maintained my tenacious grip on my status as a socially unacceptable outcast who hid behind a big sketchbook most of the day. Even though Cam could be best friends with anyone he wanted to, it's never occurred to him to dump me, and I've never been more grateful for that than I am as he helps me plan the distribution of my grandmother's left-behind things.

"You want to assembly line this?" he asks, eyeing three rows of oversized purses and satchels spread out over Grandma's bed.

"Yeah," I say. "I've got toiletries."

"I'll do leg warmers." Cam is smiling up a storm. The room is noticeably brighter and at least ten degrees cozier as a result.

"Let's do this."

We start packing the purses with Grandma's tiny soaps and shampoos, leg warmers, headbands, and sunglasses. We carefully roll up handmade shawls and scarves and stuff them in too.

"What about these mittens?" Cam asks. They're handmade by grandma from bright red yarn and have little pom poms hanging from the cuffs.

"Pack 'em," I tell him, "And any other pairs you find. There are hats somewhere too. Tons of 'em."

When we're done, the bags are bursting at the seams with personal hygiene items and warm winter wear. They stand in lines on Grandma's bed, stuffed, at attention like a bizarre little handbag army.

"We good?" Cam says, looking around at the empty space where the mess of Grandma's stuff had been strewn.

"Good," I say.

We start gathering up the handbags.

As we head for the front door, my mother comes out of the kitchen. She has a half-full glass of wine in one hand and a bottle in the other. We must have caught her midpour.

"Where are you going?" she asks. There's no way she doesn't notice that we're each carrying at least fifteen over-stuffed purses.

"To donate Grandma's things," I say. If there's an edge to my voice, fine. If it makes her feel guilty for not helping me deal with Grandma's stuff at all, even finer.

"Oh." My mom smiles a little sadly. "That's great," she says. "Camden, you're a life saver."

I roll my eyes and stomp out while Cam tells her it's no problem whatsoever.

"You ready for this, Su-Su?" Cam asks me as he starts his car.

The nickname makes me smile. When we were little, he couldn't say Sulie, so he just called me Su-Su, and our moms thought it was adorable. He still does it sometimes, and I never object. He told me once that *sous-sus* is also a ballet term, and, whenever he hears it in class, it makes him think of me. I like that, like knowing that even when he's off in his own world, one I'll never be a part of, he thinks of me.

I buckle my seatbelt and snuggle into the crocheted shawl I'm still wearing. "I'm ready," I say. And we're off.

Cam's big idea, obviously, is to pass Grandma's handbags out to the homeless women he always sees in the city on his way to and from his ballet studio. He says he's been noticing them a lot more lately because it's been so cold out since Thanksgiving, and he's been feeling really sorry for them. I know, I just know, that Grandma Nell would love this idea, so, while I admit that I did keep a larger-than-my-mother-needs-to-know-about stash of Grandma's handmade shawls and scarves and stuff for myself, passing out the rest of her belongings to people who will really appreciate and use them will be fairly easy for me. Easier than dumping them all into some anonymous church donation bin, anyway.

Charlotte is a small city and a pretty nice one too. It's not like the sidewalks are littered with homeless bodies or anything, but there are people in need just like there are in any urban center. Cam finds street parking, and we take as many of the bags as we can carry out of his trunk and start pounding the pavement.

It's not long before we see someone lying on a bus-stop bench. I'm not sure it's a woman. Cam says it doesn't matter. The person is sleeping, so we leave a packed purse next to the bench and sneak away. I'm giggling, and my heart's racing like we just got away with something.

"Come on," Cam says, expertly navigating the streets of Uptown. "This way."

Sure enough, there's a little group of three definitely disadvantaged women huddled together on the steps of a closed-for-the-weekend office building. They're wearing scratchy, institutional-looking blankets around their shoulders, and rubbing their hands together for warmth. The streetlights highlight faces full of worry lines. I hesitate as we get close, but Cam approaches them fearlessly.

"Hey," he says. "Can you help me out?"

One of the ladies eyes him almost meanly.

"You know anyone who could use some soap or warm clothing?" Cam asks them.

"Maybe," one of them says, peering at us and our handbags. The lust with which she stares at the basic necessities in our arms really touches me.

"Can I just leave a bunch of these with you?" Cam asks her, holding out five of the purses.

"Yeah, sure," another lady says, taking the bags a little too eagerly. "We know some folks."

"Thank you," Cam says.

"Yeah," I say, wanting to leave them with as much dignity as possible. "Thanks a lot."

We wander in the dark for a long time, forgetting all about dinner, distributing Grandma's things to strangers she would have converted into instant friends. One lady cries and tells us that she used to have a good, steady retail job and took care of all her bills until an illness bankrupted her and she wound up on the streets. Her story makes me cry too, and she and Cam pull me into a weird group hug. Another older lady tells us that she sleeps in a nearby shelter and takes us there so we can leave a bunch of Grandma's bags at the front desk. The woman on duty thanks us profusely and says she'll give them to everyone they have to turn away that night so that at least nobody will have to leave empty-handed. The thought of people who've already been turned away by society also being turned away by a homeless shelter has me swiping at my eyes again. One man, shivering in just a T-shirt, sees us passing out the purses and says, "Hey, man, can I get one of those too?"

"Sure," Cam tells him. "Wait. I have the perfect one." It's a medium-sized, androgynous denim backpack with black leg-warmers and a knit hat and a big bulky crocheted sweater inside.

"Cool, man," the guy says, shouldering the bag with a huge smile. He shakes our hands. "Thanks a lot."

He's got a little bucket with him, and inside is one wilted, plastic-wrapped bouquet of flowers that had obviously been discarded by a florist or a grocery store. He offers us the flowers in exchange for the bag. "Listen," he says to us, "I don't take nothin' for free, all right? I sell these. I'm a flower salesman. And I'll trade you my last bouquet for this stuff."

I take the bouquet and smile at him. I bring the flowers up to my face and inhale. There's still some perfume left in them, but I can smell some rot too. "Thank you," I tell him. "They're beautiful."

The last bag is an oversized, quilted sunflower-print bag that my grandmother had made herself. It has a soft, fuzzy handle and a smooth satin lining with a zippered pouch sewn into it that I remember filling with hotel mouthwash and a miniature hotel-issue sewing kit. The bag is one of my favorites, the most vibrant in my grandmother's collection, and, when we see a woman in tattered outerwear walking the edge of a dry-for-the-winter fountain like it's a balance beam at the Olympics and smiling to herself in an almost childlike way, I know that she should have it.

"A blessing bag!" the woman exclaims like it's the greatest thing she's ever seen. She hops off the edge of the fountain and takes the bag from us. Even though she's obviously living on the streets, her face is bright, unconcerned, happy. Her eyes are clear, captivating. "I used to make these with my girls when they were little," she tells us, clutching Grandma's purse close to her chest. "We used bags we got from the dollar store and passed them out at the soup kitchen together." She hugs the purse tightly as her eyes fill with liquid nostalgia. "I used to be a person who did for others," she says quietly.

"When you do for others, it comes back to you tenfold," Cam tells her, which I think is total bullshit. This woman passed out how many blessing bags with her kids a million years ago? And now she's just getting one crappy little bag back? How is that tenfold? I know for a fact that Cam saw that stupid saying on a poster outside the school's front office, but the woman he just unloaded it on nods and smiles sagely like Cam has just imparted some great piece of wisdom. He gives her one of his trademark big hugs and she accepts it with enthusiasm. I can't help but offer her one too.

"Here," I say and hand her the half-dead flowers I've been carrying around. Her face lights up with joy and she cradles the bouquet in her arm like a prima ballerina on opening night.

"Thank you. How beautiful," she says reverently. "Life is so beautiful!" she tells us with a girlish laugh before we part company.

"Yeah, it is," Cam agrees.

I just nod, but I have to admit that her joy is slightly contagious.

When we get back to the car, I'm exhausted. Emotionally and physically spent.

"Su-Su?" Cam says. "You OK?"

"Yeah," I tell him. "I'm just tired."

We ride in comfortable silence for a while. I snuggle into Grandma's shawl.

"Thanks, Cam," I say as we pull into our neighborhood. I know it might not seem like I have a lot sometimes, but I'm suddenly overwhelmed by a sense of gratitude for the things and people in my life. "Thanks for today."

"No problem," he says, tossing his radiant smile in my direction.

"Yeah, it was," I tell him. "It was a huge problem. A giant pain in your ass. After you rehearsed all day and everything. And you still did it anyway."

Cam laughs. "So, would you say you owe me one, then?" he asks.

"Yeah," I say. "Definitely. More than one."

"Because I kind of need a favor."

"Name it," I say. "Anything."

"Can you pick me up after rehearsal tomorrow?"

I sigh.

"Pleeeeeeeeease? My car needs an oil change, and they said it might take a while. I can get a ride from the car place to the studio, but then I'll need a ride back to pick up the car."

"What time?"

"Five o'clock?"

"I'll be there."

"I know."

Chapter Four

Five o'clock takes forever to come. I spend the day holed up in my room with a plate of soggy-but-still-delicious pastrami sandwiches and my sketchbook. I draw and draw and draw. It's the best way to keep myself from thinking.

I draw the people we met on the streets last night. The easy-going flower guy with his denim backpack, the cluster of women on the office-building steps. I draw the last lady we met, the one we gave the sunflower bag to, and that picture's the best of the bunch, I think. Her hair looks expertly wind-blown, and some of the woman's optimism and inner peace come across in her face. Her eyes look eerily alive. Sometimes, I'm weirdly good at drawing eyes.

Eventually, my hand can't help but draw Grandma Nell, and as soon as it starts happening, I want to stop it, but I can't. I have no conscious control over my pencil. I blink away tears as I draw, as her face appears on the page, not the way I'd prefer to remember her, but the way she looked at the end, the very end when she didn't even look like herself anymore—her usually radiant face twisted in agony, her once warm, bright eyes dark and distant, her gnarled fingers clutching at her bed sheets.

There are a couple other pages in my sketchbook like this that I refuse to even look at now, but it almost doesn't matter because I see those images anyway every time I close my eyes. I haven't slept through the night in a while. I finish the sketch compulsively, though I'd give anything to be able to stop myself. Then I slam the book shut on Grandma's pained expression, her tortured eyes and her twisted mouth crying out for relief from her suffering.

I'm super early to pick up Cam. I think about driving around Uptown for a while until his rehearsal lets out, but I'm not the best navigator, and I just know I'll get caught up in some kind of road-construction detour or one-way-only street mess that makes it so I can't get back to the studio on time, so I park and go inside to wait. I abhor lateness. And people who are late.

I sit in this weird waiting place between dance studios, an industrially carpeted, sparsely furnished space haunted by the ghosts of decades' worth of parents sitting still for long stretches while their outside lives passed them by. It's empty now, except for me, which means that the little kids are done for the day. As usual, Cam's hard-core older group—the preprofessionals—will be the last to leave.

I always feel weird when I have to pick Cam up from ballet for one reason or another, like everyone is wondering who the clumsy-looking nondancer girl is and why she's just sitting like a lump in the waiting room. I shift in my seat, sitting up a little straighter and trying to look just a bit more lithe and graceful…then I sigh and give up and sink back into my seat. Cam's dance friends probably wonder how on earth someone like me could even know someone like Cam every time they see us together, every time I find myself an intruder in their exclusive ballet universe. Their balletverse.

I'm wearing a heavy sweater crocheted by my grandmother as well as a handmade hat and scarf that don't necessarily match. I'm too warm, but I don't remove any layers. I take out my sketchbook and draw imaginary people waiting for imaginary dancers to finish imaginary rehearsals. I make them all look as uncomfortable and lumpish and intruderish as I feel.

Suddenly, the waiting area is buzzing as dancers in matching leotards swarm out of the big studio on the right. A herd of leggy size twos with their hair in identical buns stampedes past me. I hold my sketchbook in front of me, a shield to deflect their grace and beauty.

"Sorry you had to wait," Cam says, flinging himself into the seat next to mine as the ballerina pack disperses. He looks sweaty and tired but really, really happy. "We ran long again."

"No problem," I tell him. The overhead track lighting is like a row of mini stage lights. One of them is hitting Cam's face in a spectacular way, and I turn to a fresh page in my sketchbook and start drawing him.

"Your girlfriend is drawing you again, man," this jerk named Serge observes. He's wiping his face and neck with a towel and scowling. I swear he's wearing eye liner for no good reason.

"I'm not his girlfriend," I say. I look up from my work to glare at Serge, but my hand keeps sketching. I know the lines and planes of Cam's face so well at this point that, if my arm were suddenly severed by a marauding axe man, my disembodied hand could probably finish the drawing all on its own.

"Whatever," Serge says. "Girlfriend, groupie. She's always freaking drawing you. Doesn't it, like, annoy the piss out of you?"

Cam laughs and shrugs. I've been drawing him since I could hold a pencil. I don't think he even notices me doing it anymore.

"Nah," he says, winking at me. "Not as long as she's getting my good side."

This skinny bitch named Mia Nardone sidles up behind Cam and puts her hands on his shoulders. "Oh, come on, Cam-Cam. You don't have a bad side," she coos.

She's wrong. He does. It's his left.

Mia throws her arm around Cam's neck and presses her cheek against his and pulls out her phone. "Say cheese before I go change," she tells him.

I glance away so my involuntary eyeroll won't be too obvious. I think Mia and Cam have had sex. Cam and I don't really talk about that kind of thing; it's just a hunch I have. He acted really weird once after they went out on some big date and, even though Cam swears she's not his girlfriend, every time they're together she always has her hands all over him. I want Cam to be happy and everything, but, sometimes, their PDA is a bit much.

Cam makes this really goofy face at Mia's phone and yells, "Swiss and Gruyère!" as she takes the selfie.

"What? No picture of me?" Serge says, puffing out his chest and flexing his muscles. He's shorter than Cam but definitely ripped and really intense-looking, with a hawklike face and naturally dark hair that's only natural at the roots. He dyes the rest of it white blonde. I might even draw him sometimes when he's not around. He's the closest thing the ballet studio has to a badass, with a black cross tattooed on the side of his neck. I'm pretty sure he thinks the tat makes him look tough, but, personally, I think he looks like he was held down in an alley and vandalized by a group of overzealous Christians.

Mia humors Serge, holding up her phone again. Just as she snaps the picture, Serge makes a revolting gesture that involves his hand and his tongue.

"Gross!" Mia shouts and leans over to slap his bare upper arm hard enough to leave a red mark, but she doesn't delete the picture. She takes off toward the elevators, where she and this other goddess en pointe, Natalie, collapse in a fit of giggles, staring at the phone.

The only other senior boy in Cam's ballet group, James, comes out of the studio just in time to witness Serge's obscene gesture and shakes his head as he tosses his bag onto the seat next to Cam's, then takes a long swig of water. James is absolutely beautiful, dark-skinned with strikingly light-brown eyes and a Greek-god physique. He's also weirdly quiet and reserved, both plusses in my book. The track lighting plays off his face in an interesting way too, and, if Serge wouldn't make some stupid comment about it, I'd turn to a fresh page and start trying to capture James on paper right now. It annoys me that I can't, and I take about fifty mental photographs of James that I can refer back to later. You know, purely for artistic purposes.

Serge is staring at me staring at James, so I make a stink face at him and hunch over my sketchbook.

"You wanna get going?" Cam asks me. "The car place closes at six."

"Yeah," I say, not looking up from my drawing. "Whatever."

"Let me go throw some real pants on," Cam says, grabbing his bag. "I'll be right back."

I suddenly hate him for leaving me alone with his friends.

"That's amazing," James says, and I look up to see him gesturing toward the picture of Cam in my lap. "Your drawing? It's really beautiful."

"Thanks," I say. I feel myself overheating even more underneath all my grandma's crochet.

"You're really talented." James smiles at me and picks up his bag. He hesitates a minute and then says an awkward, "Well, see ya," to the room in general.

Serge gives him a nod and says, "Later," but I'm completely frozen and don't acknowledge him in any way as he leaves. Damn it.

I don't know why Serge isn't leaving too, but I decide not to acknowledge him in any way either, which is tough because his is one of those presences that fills up any space he's in, even one as high-ceilinged and empty as the ballet waiting room. I'm only pretending to work on my drawing now. I can't concentrate with Serge's black-hole eyes scrutinizing me.

My phone beeps, and it's a welcome distraction. Someone I know has been tagged on multiple social media sites. It's Cam. Because he's my only real friend, online and in real life, and even my phone knows this and alerts me to anything even remotely Cam-related. Mia's posted the picture she just took of them and captioned it: "Hanging with Cam after rehearsal." I think this is pretty much a lie, since she didn't really hang with him, just took the picture and left, but I shrug and toss my phone back into my bag. Cam's just seen the picture too and "liked" it, giving it a big electronic thumbs up. This seriously irks me for some reason.

"I'm starving," Cam says as he returns in his street clothes. "Wanna grab something to eat after we pick up the car?"

"Come over to my house," I tell him. "We're still drowning in pastrami."

"Excellent," Cam says with one of his huge smiles. "Let's go."

Serge watches me as I close my sketchbook and stand up.

"See you tomorrow," Cam says to him in a friendly way.

"Yeah," Serge says, not sounding super friendly. "See ya." He doesn't seem at all inclined to gather his stuff and leave the waiting area, and I have this weird feeling that I should offer him a ride and a pastrami sandwich. But I don't.

Chapter Five

"Sulie? Sulie? Miss Bingle?"

I hate my last name. Bingle. Rhymes with jingle and single. One letter off from bungle.

"Sulie!"

Cam kicks me, and I sit up straight and realize I've been zoning out in the middle of FST, Functions, Statistics, and Trigonometry, or, as a lot of the kids call it, Fucking Stupid Trig.

"Uh, yeah?" I say.

Mr. Ulstead, the teacher, looks disappointed in me. "Do you have the solution to problem five?" he asks, but he doesn't sound very hopeful.

"Um. Forty-two?"

The jerkiest kids in class snicker.

Mr. Ulstead shakes his head and asks Julia Mayhew, who rattles off a complicated equation.

I don't care that Mr. Ulstead is disappointed in me, but Cam is not-smiling in my direction as well, and I hate that. I get to work doodling in my notebook, trying to make it look like I'm taking notes.

"Are you OK?" Cam asks me for the millionth time as we stop by my locker at the end of the day.

I feel like he's been treating me with kid gloves ever since I lost it on the sidewalk in front of Tony Baloney's, and it's starting to get to me. This is one of the many, many reasons I've been finding it way easier to just bury my feelings deep inside myself. And then make sure they stay buried under a heavy layer or two of my grandmother's crochet.

"I'm fine," I tell him, tossing my books into my locker and slamming the door.

"Really?" he says. "Because you don't look fine. You look like a mess."

"Thanks." I start walking down the hall, my hands jammed into crocheted pockets.

Cam falls into step beside me. "I mean, what is this thing you're wearing, even?"

I stop and look down at myself.

"Honestly? I'm not sure. A dress?"

Cam shakes his head. "I don't think so," he says. "A big shirt? Or a tunic, maybe."

We both consider the bulky garment I'm swimming in. It's one of Grandma's, of course, but it must be one of her earlier pieces because it's ill-fitting and misshapen in places. There's a weird pattern of black-and-white spirals all over this thing that's too long to be a sweater and too short to be a dress. But I love that it has a huge hood and a kangaroo pouch in front as well as two deep side pockets. I paired it with some skinny jeans and threw on some boots and, until Cam started calling the ensemble into question, I'd thought the outfit was passable.

"And why are you wearing so many scarves?" Cam asks, tugging at a red-and-yellow fringy number around my neck.

"It's December. I'm cold."

"Bullshit. Do you really like this outfit?"

I think about this for a second.

"Screw you." I start to walk away again.

Cam doesn't let me get far. "Aren't you worried that people are going to think you're pants-on-head crazy?" he asks me.

"No," I say confidently.

"No?"

"First of all, people don't think about me one way or an-other. Second, if a cheerleader showed up dressed like this, then, yeah, she'd look crazy. But someone like me? A loner who clutches a sketchbook like a security blanket? I just look artsy."

"People think about you, Sulie," Cam says. He grabs my arm to make me stop walking and reaches for my jumble of scarves. I let him untie one of them, a scallop-edged purple number, and try not to smile as he hangs it around his own neck. "Can I pull off this look too?" he asks me with his beau-tiful smile. "What do you think? Crazy or artsy?"

Before I can answer, Jack Bramovitch shoves himself be-tween us. "Yo, Camden, what's up?" he says, holding out his fist.

"Not much," Cam says, pounding Jack's fist with his own. "What's up with you?"

"Hi, Jack," I say.

"What's up is just everything," Jack says. "Dude, listen! Huge party this weekend at my place, OK? Friday night till whenever on Sunday. My parents are going on some disgusting second honeymoon or whatever, and I'm opening the bar and firing up the hot tub. I'm lining up some sweeeeet ass too. What do you say?"

"Hey, Jack," I say.

Cam looks from me to Jack and then shakes his head. "No can do, I'm afraid. My weekend is booked solid. *The Nut-cracker.* All weekend. Seriously. Three performances a day."

"Jack," I try. "Yo."

"All weekend, bro? Harsh. That really is a *nut cracker*, huh? Get it?" He gestures toward his crotch. They both laugh these jerky laughs.

"Hello, Jack. Hi there."

"All right, dude," Jack says, clapping Cam on the shoulder. "I'll give you a pass on this one because you have to go and do your thing, but if you get a break, you come by, a'ight?"

"Definitely," Cam says. "Thanks for the invite."

"No sweat. See ya, bro."

I raise my voice a little. "Bye, Jack. Yeah. Later, dude. You total dipshit."

Cam sighs.

"Too bad you can't go to his party," I say, pulling Grandma's scarf off his neck and wrapping it back around my own where it belongs. "You'll be missing out on all that sweeeeet ass soaking in his hot tub. Not to mention the chance to have your head swirled in his toilet like he did to you in the fifth grade. Remember that?"

"Yeah," Cam says, a look of resignation settling on his face. He gazes over my shoulder, no longer willing to meet my eyes. "I remember."

"Good," I say. "For a minute there, I thought I was the only one."

Cam, wisely, decides to change the subject. "So you're coming on Friday, right? Opening night?"

"Of course I am," I say.

I actually hate *The* freaking *Nutcracker* because it's just stupid that all those sweets come to life and dance. I mean, seriously, what's even a little bit appetizing about that? I've already seen the show a million times too, at least once a year starting back when Cam was just a little stripey-panted Polichinelle running out from under some big dude's skirt, but I've never missed one of Cam's opening nights, and, this year, he's dancing the best part, the Sugar Plum Fairy's Cavalier, so, yeah, of course I'm going to be in the audience.

"OK," he says. "I'm picking up the tickets tonight. I'll drop yours off for you, all right? Because my Friday is going to be nuts."

"Not as nuts as it could have been soaking in Jack Bramovitch's hot tub. Or toilet."

Cam rolls his eyes. "I have to go," he says. He leans in to give me a weird little one-armed hug and kisses me on the head even though it makes me flinch. "God, you're burning up!" he says over his shoulder as he starts off down the hallway. "Take off some scarves, Sulie. For real." His smile looks really fake, and it makes me shiver under all my knitwear.

Chapter Six

The kids at school used to give Cam a hard time about the ballet thing. It started sometime in elementary school as clear social groups began to form and the self-selected jocks grew into their natural, Darwin-justified roles of bullying everyone who doesn't think sports are the end-all, be-all of human existence. They just teased Cam at first, calling him Twinkle Toes and Ballet Boy and other stupid shit that he mostly managed to laugh off. But then they started pushing him around and calling his boy/manhood into question loudly and often. The violence escalated, with Cam being shoved into lockers, knocked out of his cafeteria seat, and pegged half to death with dodge balls in gym class. Then, of course, there was the famous toilet-dunking by none other than hot-tubbin' Jack Bramovitch.

I tried to stick up for Cam; I really did. But since I'm pretty much invisible, it didn't help very much. After the toilet thing, I kicked Jack Bramovitch in the nuts after school, and even though he was bent double and I knew it had to hurt, he and his friends all just laughed at me as I ran away from them and jumped onto my bus.

Anyway, Cam was just as unpopular as I was—although, often to his dismay, not as invisible—until the very end of middle school when he signed up to dance a solo in the school talent show. When he took the stage in his stretchy dance-denim jeans and tight white T-shirt, so many people were screaming so many mean things at him, I don't even know how he heard his music start. But he did, and he started to dance. And, within seconds, the audience fell silent as the haters, one by one, realized what it was they were seeing.

It wasn't tendus and plies and boring *Nutcracker* crap. Cam was athletic and powerful and exciting up there. The dance, set to some fairly hardcore hip-hop music that I know for a fact Cam didn't even like, wasn't especially artistic. It was a little showboaty, actually, if you ask me, full of fast turns and huge jumps and even a backflip. Some of the kicks looked more like they belonged in a martial arts dojo than a ballet studio, but the routine was mesmerizing. Cam was mesmerizing. And when the song ended and he stood center stage, breathless, the utter silence lasted one more awkward moment, and then the crowd went wild. Even the kids who'd spent years and years torturing Cam were on their feet applauding him, nodding their respect, pumping their fists in his honor. In the space of two minutes, half the student body had fallen in love with him, and the other half had started thinking they should maybe hit the gym a little harder to catch up to that crazy son-ofabitch Cam McLaren.

And that was the end of Cam's quasi loserhood and the beginning of his whole new life as a high school superstar.

I try not to think about my own role in Cam's rise to popularity because it makes me feel really guilty. I'd told him not to do the talent show, begged him not to give the bullies anything else they could use against him. I told him dancing in front of the whole school was a no-good, awful, terribad idea that would doom him to a high school career marked by mockery, locker-room wedgies, and black eyes.

I'd like to think I was afraid of what would have happened if the other kids hadn't liked Cam's dancing. But maybe, having seen for myself how beautiful and talented Cam was, I was actually more afraid of what would happen if they loved it. Which, of course, they did. And I was happy for Cam. I really was. But my stomach dropped just a little as I tried not to think about what would happen if all of the other, cooler, smarter, richer kids applauding him suddenly wanted to be Cam's friends too.

I'm still thinking about Jack Bramovitch when Cam comes by to drop off my *Nutcracker* ticket. It's late, and I'm already in my flannel pajamas and one of Grandma's shawls, sitting up in bed with my sketchbook, but my mom lets him in anyway. He looks really beat. I can tell he just got out of rehearsal; he smells like dry sweat and dirty leather ballet slippers.

"Here," he says, holding out an envelope to me. I assume my ticket's inside.

"Thanks," I say. "I can't wait to see it."

Cam smiles. He's tired, so it doesn't have its usual wattage, but it's genuine, at least.

"Yes, you can," he says. "You hate *The Nutcracker*."

"What? I do not! Nobody hates *The Nutcracker*."

Cam laughs. "You do, and I love you for seeing it every year anyway."

"OK," I say. "Well, as ballet plots go, it's not my favorite, but you are, so I really can't wait to watch."

"Thanks."

"Cam, listen," I say. "I'm sorry for my attitude this afternoon. At school? About Jack and bringing up the toilet and everything? I'm really sorry."

"It's OK," Cam says. He pauses in a way that makes me think it's not really all that OK with him, actually. "Honestly, Sulie, I wish I were brave enough not to be friends with those guys, you know? But it's just so much easier to humor them than it is to have my head flushed on a regular basis."

"I get that. Yeah."

"Listen," Cam says. "I know it's lame compared to sweeeeet ass in a hot tub or whatever, but a bunch of us are going out for pizza after the show on Friday. You should come."

"No, thanks."

"I'd like it if you came," he says.

I try to think of a reason I can't.

Cam picks up my sketchbook and points to the drawing I was working on. "*He'll* be there," he says with a devilish grin and a flick of his eyebrows.

I blush and grab my sketchbook. I'd been drawing James from memory.

"Really, Sulie, he's nice."

James moved here less than a year ago, so he hasn't been dancing with Cam and the rest of the group forever and ever, and everyone's still kind of getting to know him.

"James is really smart," Cam continues, "and he does some volunteer work... I like him. I think you guys would really get along. Come out with us. I'll try to work it so you get to sit together."

"OK," I say, but I feel embarrassed for some reason. Maybe because my best friend has to try to rustle up dates for unpopular me. I look down at my sketchbook and see James's beautiful face staring back at me, and that actually makes me blush harder.

Cam leaves, and I keep thinking about him. And about James. And about how I've never had a boyfriend except for this one guy I met at a summer art camp who kissed me right before we both went off to different high schools, certain never to see one another again. I hadn't even enjoyed the experience because the guy had been eating a banana right before it happened, and I didn't think he tasted sexy at all. I wonder what would happen if I kissed James at the pizza parlor. Would the taste of pepperoni ruin it, or would I end up wanting to devour him whole?

Chapter Seven

Cam's super busy with last-minute *Nutcracker* shit all week, so I'm super lonely. The house is quiet without Grandma Nell in it, and the ache in my core from missing her feels like the worst kind of hunger pains. I go into the bathroom and try to scavenge some hair out of Grandma's hairbrush; my mother still hasn't thought to clean out her bathroom drawer. I think that if I can just get a taste of Grandma, just make her a little more a part of me, I won't feel so left-behind, so lost. But the hair in her brush has gone stale; it tastes of dust and the sadness of being forgotten. There's nothing left of my grandmother in it. It's inanimate, lifeless, dead. I chew on it for a while, but can't bring myself to swallow, don't want anything so depressing inside of me, so I end up spitting out this huge hairball, which makes me gag, which makes me vomit. After I brush my teeth, I sneak back to my room feeling even worse.

I pretty much spend all my non-school time in my room. I make a nest out of some of Grandma's shawls and sweaters in the middle of my bed and then use a bunch of other shawls and ponchos as a cover, so I'm basically swaddled in crochet as much as possible, and that helps. That and my sketchbook full of interesting people who keep me company. It's nice to talk with them, actually. When they start to talk back, though, I question some of my decisions about how to spend my alone time. I'm very careful to avoid glimpsing the drawings of near-death Grandma, and I don't try to draw her anymore.

My mother hosts her monthly single-mom support group at our house on Wednesday, a make-up meeting since she had to cancel the one that was supposed to take place the night my grandmother had the audacity to die. Some of the newer group members bring my mom flowers and casseroles and tell her how sorry they are for her loss. The ones who've known her the longest bring her bottles of wine and don't try to comfort her at all.

Even though I huddle inside my crochet pile, our house is pretty small, and I can hear every stupid thing these ladies say. Why my mother has been meeting with them for, like, ten years is so beyond me. First, her being a single mom is a total crock of shit. Yeah, my dad left when I was really little, but Grandma Nell moved right in, so my mom has never really been on her own, not for a minute. Plus, it's not like I'm in diapers anymore. I pretty much just do my own thing. Second, the group members don't even talk about single-mom stuff like child support or substitute male role models for their kids. As far as I can tell, every word out of their mouths is about some stupid book one of them read and is happy to summarize for the group to save the other members the trouble of actually cracking a book's spine or some guy someone is dating—probably a middle-aged balding fellow—who really *gets* it, who's meeting the group member where she *is* in life or how someone's ungrateful kid is disappointing them yet again by, like, basically just being a kid. In my eavesdropping experience, my mother's contributions to the group tend to be sympathetic monosyllables, but tonight's different, as the spotlight's on her and her recent loss.

"It's been really hard," she says when someone asks her how she's holding up. "I mean, dealing with all Mom's things? Cleaning out her closet? It about put me over the edge."

"You poor thing."

"Hang in there, Laurel."

"You were a good daughter, letting her live here. Letting her stay here instead of sending her to that hospice house. A good daughter right till the end."

"And I don't know *what* to do with Sulie," my mom continues. "I mean, she's taking it hard, but come on. We knew this was coming. It shouldn't have been a shock." My mother snorts. "Seriously, how inconvenient is it for her to decide that *now* is the time to turn into a surly, antagonistic teenager?"

I fume silently, thinking how cathartic it might be to run out into the living room and yell at everyone there, tell them all that I'm a legal adult, thank you very much, and can act however I'd like to in the wake of my beloved grandmother's death, that I'm going to start my own support group for eighteen-year-olds with infantile, whiny mothers.

I don't do that, though.

As the other group members murmur their agreement that my feelings are, indeed, a huge inconvenience for my mother, the doorbell rings, and I scream, "I'll get it!" and jump out of my cozy nest so they know I can hear everything in my room.

I figure it's going to be another one of my mom's group members come to whine and wine, so I might make a really stupid, shocked face when I fling the door open and see an angry-looking Black girl standing on our front porch, glaring at me.

She's wearing a gray, puffy jacket zipped protectively up to her chin. Her mouth is set in a hard line, and she narrows her unblinking eyes at me as she speaks. "Nell Foster?"

"Um, no?" I say, pulling one of Grandma's shawls around me in self-defense.

"Well, is she here?" The girl exhales impatiently through her nose so that her nostrils flare.

I'm terrified to say no, but I tell the truth. "She died. She's dead."

"Oh." Some of the anger leaves the girl's face, and she de-flates a little bit. "Um, I'm sorry," she says, blinking and taking a half step backward.

"She was my grandma," I tell her. I don't know why. Maybe just because I want everyone in the whole world to know we were related. "She just passed last week."

"Shit," the girl says. "I'm, like, really sorry." She shifts from foot to foot and looks away.

"Can I help you with something?" I try.

"No. I don't know."

We just stand there a minute, feeling awkward for our own reasons.

"Here." The girl thrusts something into my hands, and I clutch at it, startled. It's one of Grandma's purses, one of the ones Cam and I had made into blessing bags and passed out in Uptown. It's the sunflower-print one, the one Grandma had made herself.

"Hey!" I say. "Grandma's purse!"

"Yeah," the girl says. "Well, now you have it back. There wasn't anything valuable left in it when I got it, I swear." She turns to leave.

"Wait. What?"

"And I don't know the whole story," the girl says, stopping and turning back toward me. "OK? I really don't. The cops just said my mom had this on her when she passed, and I wanted to make sure it got returned to its rightful owner. All right? Like I said, I don't know the whole story, but I know I don't come from any family of thieves, OK? So, whatever happened happened, and now you have the bag back just the way I found it."

"Thieves?"

"You heard me. My people don't steal, all right?"

"All right."

The girl walks away as I hold the bag to my chest. Something dawns on me. "Did you say the woman who had this bag passed away?" I call after her. "Died?"

"Yeah." The girl stops, but she doesn't turn around.

"Did she have, like, long salt-and-pepper hair and light-brown eyes and, like, a whole lot of optimism?"

"Yeah, she did." The girl turns around, incredulous. "Did you know her?"

"No," I say. "I mean, I think I met her once."

I tell the girl about my grandma dying, tearing up a little, but holding myself together by clutching the sunflower purse like a teddy bear. I tell her about my mom pulling Grandma's stuff out of the closet and tossing it on the floor and about me being at a total loss as to what to do with it and about Cam coming up with the blessing bag idea and about meeting the optimistic lady in the street and giving her the purse.

Now, the girl is tearing up.

"She was my mother," she says. "That was my mom."

The girl's name is Brandi, and her mom suffered from dementia and sometimes wandered away and lived on the streets for long periods of time. "She wasn't homeless, OK?" Brandi tells me. "We would look for her like crazy every time she disappeared. She had a home. She had a family! She would just, like, forget herself for a while or whatever. Forget all of us too, I guess." Brandi can't be much older than I am, but she seems almost middle-aged to me. She's already had to be a parent to her own mom. My heart breaks for her. "When they called to tell us they'd found her body, it was a total shock and, also? At the same time? Totally what I always thought would happen." Brandi's crying unapologetically now. "And then they gave us her stuff, and there was this purse in there with her coat and her hat, and none of us recognized the bag, so I went through it, and I found some Senior Stars thing with the name Nell Foster on it, and I figured, 'Oh, great. Now Mom died a thief too.'"

"No," I tell her. "No. It wasn't like that."

"I'm so relieved." She sobs. "You have no idea. My mom was a great lady. She really was. She wouldn't have stolen a thing in her right mind. She was…good."

"I know," I say. "I could tell. And you know what? She didn't forget all of you."

"What?"

"The night I met her? She talked about making blessing bags with her girls from bags you bought at the dollar store and passing them out at the soup kitchen. She remembered you. At least some long-ago version of you."

Brandi sinks to our sidewalk and cries, and I kneel next to

her and put a flimsy arm around her and pat her on the back a little and say absolutely nothing useful and feel terribly, horribly inadequate.

When Brandi, at long last, sniffles and stands up, I try to hand her the sunflower purse, and she says, "No, keep it. It was your grandmother's. Thank you. Thank you for what you did, for doing something nice for my mom in her last days."

"Wait," I tell her. "Don't go yet." I dash back into the house and grab my sketchbook. I rip out the drawing of Brandi's mom and run with it to the front lawn. "Here," I say, breathless. "I drew this right after I met your mom."

Brandi starts sobbing all over again. "Oh my God!" she says. "It's her, and it isn't, you know? Like, the crazy hair and the old hat are this whole part of her I didn't really get. But her eyes? Damn, girl! That's my mom looking at me! That's my mom."

Brandi and I hug and trade contact info. She works part-time at this place called Mission Possible that helps people on the streets transition to jobs and permanent housing. She says I should give her a call if I want to get involved, help even more people like I helped her mom.

"Thanks," I tell her. "I'll think about it."

When I go back inside, my mom's support group has stopped supporting one another and started just plain old drinking.

"Who was that at the door?" my mother asks me.

"Nobody," I tell her because I think she still thinks Grandma's handbags are all piled up in the church-store junk bin up the street, as empty and devoid of purpose as I feel.

Chapter Eight

I want to tell Cam about Brandi and her dead mother and the sunflower purse, but it doesn't seem like the kind of thing you just mention in between classes. ("Oh, by the way, that lady we met? The one you hugged and swapped philosophies of life with? She kicked it on the street the other day. See you after biology!")

After school, Cam has *Nutcracker* rehearsals, and then he has to come home and do all his homework too. He's determined to finish his high school career with a perfect four-point-oh. I try to catch him Thursday evening. I stop by his house with my copy of *Jane Eyre* for our English class. I read ahead a few weeks ago and had actually done a pretty thorough job of highlighting key points and making all kinds of notes in the margins. I want to give it to Cam because I'm pretty sure I'm not going to open it again this semester and because I think it will help him skim through the night's required chapters. Cam isn't home, though, which shouldn't be a huge surprise, but it makes me feel sad anyway.

Cam has two moms. Some people think that's kind of weird, but it doesn't faze me. For one thing, that's just always been his family. For another, up until pretty recently, I've lived alone with two women as well. In fact, neither Cam nor I would know what to do with a father figure if we tripped over one.

Cam's moms answer the door together, which is both cute and kind of annoying. They let me in and say I should leave the book in Cam's room for him, which I do, but being in there without him makes me miss him so much it physically hurts, so I toss the book on his bed without even leaving a note or anything. I pull the heavy shawl I'm wearing around me as tight as I can and head for the door.

On my way past the dresser, I see Cam's little black bag full of boys' beauty products. Manly-smelling deodorant, razors, hair crap. There's a nail clipper sticking out of the bag, and, as my eye falls on it, I see just the tiniest sliver of a nail clipping trapped between its small metal jaws. Something about the way this little piece of larger-than-life Cam has been forgotten and neglected tugs at me, draws me in. I can't just let it languish there on the dresser, let it eventually be swept into the trash or vacuumed away, gone forever, never to return. Before I can give it too much thought, before either of Cam's mothers has a chance to start wondering what's taking me so long, I pick up the nail clipper and tap that little sliver of Cam out into my hand. And then I eat it.

When I get home, I feel less lonely in some ways but more lonely in others. I reach for my sketchbook and see the jagged edge where I ripped out the picture of Brandi's mom. I think about giving Brandi a call, but I don't know what I would say that could possibly be of any interest to her. I think about drawing Brandi, but I don't want to. I only saw her angry and sad, and I don't want to spend the whole night staring at a picture of someone who looks the way I feel.

I go online but then wish I hadn't because Mia's tagged Cam in another picture. They're both drenched in sweat and making exaggeratedly tired faces at her camera, clutching bottles of water. "Me and my cavalier—final rehearsal!" she wrote. Did I mention that Mia's the Sugar Plum Fairy? No? It must have slipped my mind. Because I definitely haven't been *intentionally* not thinking about all the extra time she's been spending in Cam's arms while I curl up alone in my pile of old crochet.

I'm going to have to start washing some of it soon, I think. The crochet. It might be starting to smell a little.

Around midnight, I get a text from Cam that says, "Did you leave a book on my pillow?"

I write back that I did and tell him why.

"Can you just summarize the chapters for me when we get to school?" he asks. "I'm beat."

"Sure," I type. "How was rehearsal?"

"Good," he says.

"Good," I say and add a little smiley face.

It is good. Very, very good. I want his rehearsals to be good. Only a total bitch would hope that Mia was annoying him by stepping on his toes with her hard pointe shoes the whole time. Or kicking him in the balls with a misplaced arabesque. Or accidentally farting in his face when he lifted her in the air. Or breaking her own ankle with a clumsily landed grand jeté. I sigh almost wistfully at the thought. Almost immediately, I'm appalled at myself. Of course, I'm very, very glad that nothing like that happened. Of course I am.

"Life is so beautiful!" Cam types, adding a whole series of his own smiley faces.

I know he's thinking back to the night we handed out Grandma's bags, quoting Brandi's mom, and I want, again, to tell him how her story ended, but it's something that needs to be talked about, not texted about, and before I can dial his number, I see another message from him that says, "I'm so tired. Turning in now. 'Night!"

"'Night," I type back, but I'm not tired at all. I don't go to sleep. I just curl up in my crochet nest and wait for morning.

Chapter Nine

I meet Cam's moms in the theater lobby on Friday night. Cam calls both of them Mom, but when he needs to differentiate between them, he refers to them as Mom Kelly and Mom Rachel. It avoids a lot of confusion.

Mom Kelly is petite and blonde and high-strung and always seems a little breathless. She sells pharmaceuticals out of a little black suitcase on wheels, so she's always wearing nice little skirt suits and teetering around on these Barbie-doll high heels to impress the doctors she meets. It thrills me to no end to think that the prescriptions our doctors write might be based more on the shortness of Mom Kelly's skirt than it is on the effectiveness and safety of the medications she sells, but whatever. It's not her fault. She's just working the system.

As soon as I enter the theater lobby, Mom Kelly rushes to greet me like a long-lost friend even though I just saw her the night before. She flings herself at me in such an enthusiastic way that my only choices are to catch her up in a huge hug or sidestep her and watch her go sprawling. I suck it up and take the hug.

Mom Rachel is a brunette and a little more laid-back. She wears flats to her wife's high heels and takes her time crossing the crowded lobby to give me a much gentler, less coerced hug and tell me she likes my scarf. It's one of Grandma's, of course. I wore my favorite long black skirt for my big night out at the theater, but I couldn't help wearing one of grandma's sweaters, a crocheted vest, and a pretty black-and-hot-pink ruffled scarf too. For good measure, I've pinned one of Grandma's sparkly brooches—a crystal-encrusted star—to the scarf, right where it's knotted at my throat.

We go into the theater and find our seats. I flip through my program, looking at all the tiny little black-and-white head-shots of the dancers. As a senior, it's Cam's last *Nutcracker* (thank God), so he gets to write a little blurb next to his picture. I almost tear up when I read it. He thanks Renee, the director of his dance academy, his favorite teacher, Joshua, and all his classmates for their guidance and support. He notes that his moms are amazing and he loves them both, and then, right at the end, where probably no one but me will ever read it, he adds, "And thank you to Sulie, who doesn't even like ballet but always claps the loudest."

I flip through a little bit to see what some of the other grad-uating-and-moving-on dancers wrote. Mia thanks everyone for all the *Nutcracker* memories, especially her bae, Cam, the best pas de deux partner ever, which almost makes me barf. Her friend Natalie feels inspired by her teachers and then lists about twenty relatives that she claims got her to where she is today (which, it's not my job to point out to her, is just a community-theater stage that her tuition-based dance academy rented for the weekend). James thanks everyone for welcoming him into the academy family this year, and Serge's blurb space is blank. Apparently, he has nothing nice to say to anyone.

I'm so wrapped up in my program that I almost don't notice that Mom Kelly is on the verge of one of her preshow freak-outs. She danced when she was younger, and she takes the whole thing very seriously. She gets way more nervous than Cam does whenever he performs. Tonight, she seems to be freaking out about his hair.

"What if that new hair gel I bought him isn't strong enough?" she says. "I knew he should have gotten a haircut before opening night!"

"Relax, Kelly," Mom Rachel says. "His hair looked fine to-day."

"Yeah, when he was just standing still. But what about when he's dancing? If it flops in his face during that fouetté sequence in his solo, it will be so distracting!" Mom Kelly picks up her purse and starts to stand up. "I'd better go check on him."

Mom Rachel never took ballet. She played rugby in college. She puts a hand on Mom Kelly's arm, applying just enough pressure to convince her to sink back down into her seat. "Leave the kid alone," she says. "He can style his own hair."

"Look," I say, holding out my program. "Cam mentions you in here."

"Oh!" Mom Kelly grabs the program and skims the blurb, her eyes shining. "Isn't that sweet? Rachel?" She looks at her wife. "Isn't he the sweetest kid ever?" She reads and rereads her son's kind words, Cam's hair quickly forgotten.

Mom Rachel gives me a little thank-you nod and a conspir-atory smile as the houselights finally dim.

This year's dance-academy *Nutcracker* is exactly like every one before it, but it feels different, too, knowing that I'm watching it for the last time. Cam plans to have a long professional ballet career, and I hope he does, so he'll probably dance in other *Nutcrackers* in other places in much bigger theaters where the upholstery on the seats isn't worn quite so thin, and I plan to go to all of them. Seriously. But this is the last time I'll see this particular production with its wooden Christmas tree that "grows" when a not-as-invisible-as-everyone-pretends-it-is wire lifts it up out of the stage and its faux-fur-covered Mouse King head that's seen better days and its glittering Land of the Sweets scenery that a bunch of the moms made by hand a million years ago and retouch with extra glitter every December.

The younger kids always really impress me, and this year is no exception. As I admire their talent and self-discipline, I also remember Cam dancing some of those other parts. This year, his big dances don't happen until Act II, but, in the past, he's been a party-scene kid and the Nutcracker Prince and the naughty brother Fritz and a dancing doll and a mouse. I glance over at Cam's moms, and I can see that they're thinking about all of this too. Their hands are clasped together on their shared armrest.

Objectively speaking, I can tell that the dancing is all really good. Serge plays the sketchy Herr Drosselmeyer and does a great job with all his character's weird pantomime, elevating creepiness to an art form. He also comes back later as the super-intense Russian dancer with a bunch of powerful kicks and jumps. Serge covers his tattoo with makeup when he performs and slicks back his white-blonde hair so that he looks much more like the rest of the ballet boys on stage, much more normal, than he does in real life.

James is a beautiful Snow King and a nice-and-limber Arabian soloist in nothing but a pair of rippling gold lamé pants and rippling muscles to match. He really is just absolutely gorgeous. Natalie is James's Snow Queen, and she also dances the Spanish dance in a long skirt and a mantilla, waving a black lace fan.

Obviously, Mia is dancing perfection as the Sugar Plum Fairy with her stupid little sparkly crown and her almost laughably big, purple tutu, but I give Cam most of the credit because everyone knows that a ballerina's partner can make or break her performance.

Mostly, while they're dancing, I just watch Cam. And when it's time for his solo, he really owns the entire stage. His jumps are magnificent, and his turns are fast and sure. I do think I notice some hair floppage during what must be his big fouetté sequence, but the audience bursts into spontaneous applause as he nails turn after turn, so I don't think it's too distracting. The bulge in the front of Cam's tights, though, is another matter. I'm used to seeing him in these skin-tight costumes, so sometimes it doesn't even register with me, but once in a while it'll catch my eye, and I'll just fixate on it, no matter how much I try not to. Obviously, this wasn't an issue back when he was just a little dancing mouse, but the Sugar Plum Cavalier costume is on a whole other level. I'd say I'm a horrible, low-brow obsessed audience member, but, *come on*. Those tights leave just nothing to the imagination. This is probably why I've never once sketched Cam in his dancewear. I would definitely blush to death when I got to the crotch.

When the show's over, I wait in the hallway with Cam's moms and about a million other elated parents while the dancers cover their crotch bulges with warm-up pants and slide their tired feet into comforting puffy boots or slippers.

When Cam comes out of the dressing room, he's practically mobbed. Everyone wants to tell him how amazing he was, how extraordinary his fouettés were, how much they've enjoyed watching him all these years. Cam smiles at all of his admirers and has to shake a bunch of hands and give a bunch of hugs before he can make his way over to us. When he gets within striking distance, Mom Kelly squeals and launches herself at him. He laughs, catching her and lifting her off the ground, and she jabbers excitedly into his ear so that only he can make out what she's saying before she kisses him on the cheek. Whatever she's said to him has made his smile even brighter. When he sets her down, Mom Rachel takes her turn telling Cam how great he was and holding him tight.

"That failli assemblé thing across the stage?" she says. "Phenomenal! You looked like you were flying!" I think she's just showing off that she knows some of the lingo.

Finally, it's my turn to congratulate Cam, but I don't really know what to say. "You kicked ass," I tell him. "Seriously. I'm so proud to know you." I know he wants a hug, so I give him one even though it makes me feel kind of awkward, especially in front of his moms.

"Thanks," he says to me. "Thanks for coming." That's the thing with Cam. He doesn't really need me to tell him he's a good dancer; he knows he is. He doesn't care if I know his fouetté from his tour jeté or if I think his hair was too floppy. It just really means something to him that I showed up.

Cam's moms are in the mood to celebrate and, for a minute, I think we might get out of the pizza thing with his friends. But

Cam reminds his moms that he has plans, and Mom Kelly says, "Oh, of course! Cast party! Right. You have to go! Of course." So, she and Mom Rachel do a little more hugging and a little more congratulating and then take off for some new dessert bar they just heard about.

"Just let me take off the rest of my makeup and change," Cam says to me. "And then we can go." Cam wears makeup on stage, OK? All dancers do it. It's no big deal. "Are you driving?" he asks. "Or am I?"

"You are," I tell him. "I had my mom drop me off."

"Good thinking," he says. "Then we don't have to come back for your car."

"Yeah," I say. "That. And, also, if I had my own wheels right now, I'd probably take off for that cake shop with your moms and leave you here, and I'm trying really hard not to be a shitty friend."

Cam smiles at me. He's on top of the world right now. He's really never more *Cam* than he is after a great performance. "Don't worry, Sulie," he says. "We're going to have fun."

Chapter Ten

We do, I guess. Have fun. The pizza party isn't as torturous as I thought it would be, and Cam keeps his word about hooking me up with a seat next to James. As soon as James walks into the restaurant, Cam flags him down.

"Sit with us," Cam says. "Here." He vacates the seat next to mine and gestures for James to take it. Then he sits across from us.

James doesn't wrinkle up his nose at me and my ruffled scarf or look especially unhappy as he sits down. Actually, he looks kind of pleased and says a shy, "Hi," to me. I take it as a good sign.

"Hi," I say back. Wow. I am really nailing this hitting-on-a-guy thing. I can't believe I don't have, like, fifty boyfriends.

"You remember Sulie, right?" Cam says.

"Of course," James says. "The artist. And didn't you come out with us after Dancing in the Park last month?"

"Yup. That was me."

God.

Cam grins.

I pull my grandma's vest tight around my middle.

Cam winds up acting as the de facto host of the party since the pizza-parlor staff is overwhelmed by the number of dancers that have descended on the place at once. He's bouncing up and down, taking orders, trying to convince all the vegans to sit together so they can all share the same cheese-free, cauliflower-crust veggie pie, and smiling up a storm. When he's not trying to put the pizza-joint waiters out of a job, he's busy working to keep Mia from strangling him to death as she apparently *cannot*, to save her life, keep from wrapping all of her available limbs around him all the time.

I sip the Coke Cam puts in front of me before rushing off to find a side salad for Mia, who's complaining loudly that pizza has too many calories and that even one bite of mozzarella cheese would ruin her for life. I look around, hoping Cam comes back and sits down soon. I'm not the only outsider, but just a few of the other dancers have brought boyfriends or cousins or sisters along. Nobody but Cam brought a neurotic neighbor dressed like yarn is on its way out of style. I can tell who the other interlopers are because, like me, they don't have buns in their hair or wear comfy warm-up suits to soothe their tired muscles.

"So, um," I say to James. Then, I take another sip of my Coke. "Great performance tonight."

"Thanks," he says, smiling a little shyly.

"Yeah. Um. You were really, like, good."

"Thank you." His blush deepens, and I see him glance across the room at Cam, who is passing around extra napkins. He's probably looking for somebody to save him from having to talk to me.

"Those Arabian pants were like…whew. Those were some pants." I drink more soda. I wonder if it's possible to drown yourself in a soft-drink glass.

But James laughs, and I feel myself relax just a little.

"Yeah," he says. "Those pants! I mean, I've been to the Middle East, and, I promise you, nobody's running around in shiny gold Hammer pants over there."

Now it's my turn to laugh.

"At least I wasn't Chinese this year," he says. "That slanty eye makeup and goofy choreography needs a serious, culturally sensitive update."

James and I end up talking about his trip to the Mideast and the ballet school he went to before this one. He teaches dance to at-risk youth in his spare time, and we talk about that too. He wants to know about my sketching, but there isn't much to tell except it's like my oxygen, which he totally gets because he says that's what ballet is for him. And, of course, he wants to know how I know Cam, and, even though it might be selling Cam out a bit, I go ahead and tell him some classic Cam stories—nothing too embarrassing—like the time Cam swallowed a seashell on a day-camp trip to the beach and our whole camp group had to sit in the emergency room while he got X-rayed and the time he tried to save an injured squirrel in my back yard, and the squirrel bit him, and he ended up having to get rabies shots. I know Cam can overhear us, but I don't think he disapproves because he keeps bringing us more pizza and smiling and refilling our Cokes from a big, sweaty pitcher.

I think James and I are hitting it off really well. As the party winds down, though, he gets up to use the bathroom and Serge slithers into his seat. He's *definitely* wearing eye liner, though I guess it could be left over from the show.

"Is it true?" he asks me. "What Camden wrote in the program about you? Is it true that you don't like ballet?"

I shrug and look around for rescue. Cam is completely occupied with Mia, though.

Serge just stares at me, waiting for an answer. He blinks a lot less than most people.

"I guess," I say.

"You guess?" His heavily lined eyes bore holes in me.

"Yeah. I mean, I like that you all do it and whatever, but it's not really my thing."

"But you come all the time. I've seen you at every show."

"Yeah, well." I shrug and pull Grandma's crochet tight around me. "I like watching Cam. He's amazing."

"And what about me?"

"You?"

"Don't I amaze you?"

"What?" Is he really fishing for compliments here?

"On stage. I'm amazing too."

Seriously? I look around the pizza parlor, hoping to catch Cam's eye. How is he missing this right now?

"Uh, yeah," I finally manage to say. "You were really good as the scary godfather or whatever tonight."

"Drosselmeyer? He doesn't even really dance."

James comes back from the bathroom, but Serge doesn't relinquish his seat, and James doesn't ask him to. He just says that he has to get going and that they have to be back on stage pretty early tomorrow and everything. His goodbye is nothing special. It's a "Bye, Sulie," and that's all.

Suddenly, I'm tired, and I want my crochet nest.

"I'm going to grab a crow bar and pry Cam away from Mia so we can get going too," I say and stand up.

Serge stands up with me and grabs my arm. I'm very glad

there's a thick layer of crochet between his fingers and my flesh.

"You know you're wasting your time, right?" Serge says. "With James?"

I blush from my hairline all the way down into my ruffled scarf. Did everyone in the entire restaurant notice me flirting? And notice how bad I am at it? I look around.

The dancers who are left all seem really absorbed in their own conversations. Natalie is showing off, doing a split between two wobbly pizza-parlor chairs while some of the other dancers egg her on. Nobody is looking at me.

Serge lets go of my arm. He picks up my half-drunk Coke and makes a big show of finishing it without taking his eyes off mine. "He's into Camden," he says and wipes his mouth with the back of his hand. "James has a monster crush on Camden."

Serge leaves without saying goodbye to anyone or making any excuses about early call times tomorrow.

Cam's still smiling a hundred-watt smile as we drive home together. "So, you and James, huh?" he says. "Looked like it was going really well."

I tell him what Serge said. His smile becomes a look of shock. We swerve, almost driving off the road.

"Oh my God," he says. "This explains so much. I feel so stupid."

"Don't," I tell him.

"Really, Su-Su, I'm so sorry. He asked me a couple different times if you were my girlfriend. I thought he liked you."

"He doesn't."

"I'm such an ass. I think I've been leading him on! Tonight, I was all like, 'Hey! Sit with us!' I gave him my chair."

"Yeah," I say. "You're practically engaged."

"No, but there's other stuff too," Cam says morosely. "Like in rehearsal the other day, I was admiring his legs!"

"What?"

"Like, his calves. They're really…muscular. And he's a crazy-powerful jumper. And I was telling him how amazing his calves were and asking him all about his gym routine. And then I said we should work out together sometime!"

"OK," I say. "That's pretty bad."

"What should I do?" he asks.

"Nothing."

"Should I say something?"

"No."

"No?"

"No. I mean, James wasn't interested in me tonight, but he didn't make some big speech about it. He wasn't all like, 'Hey, Sulie, I just want to make sure you know that I can only ever like you as a friend,' or whatever."

"Yeah, but he also didn't run his hands all over your legs and invite himself into your workout routine."

"He sees you with Mia."

"Mia?"

"The human octopus usually attached to you at the hip?"

"You think he thinks we're a thing?"

"Aren't you?"

"No." Cam casts a furtive glance in my direction and then shifts his eyes back to the road. "Well. I mean. No!"

"He'll figure it out, Cam. One way or another, he'll eventually realize that you're never going to like him back. And that sucks, and it might make him feel like crap, but nobody besides him will really care, and he will just have to live with it and move on."

"That seems harsh."

I snuggle a little deeper into my knitwear, pull my knees up to my chest and stare out the window into the darkness.

"It is."

Chapter Eleven

When I get home, my mother's sitting at the kitchen table in front of a glass of wine and a cardboard box.

"Sulie," she says. She sounds surprised to see me. Which is weird because I'm home right when I said I would be.

"Hi," I say.

"Hi," she says. Then she laughs. I know this isn't her first glass of wine tonight. "How was the show?"

"Oh," I say, "good. It was really good."

"That's good." My mom nods thoughtfully. "I should have gone with you. It's been a while since I've seen Camden perform."

"That's OK," I say. "You've had a lot going on with Grandma and everything."

"That I have," she says, even though she hasn't, really. I mean, she didn't have to plan her mother's funeral or dispose of her things. She taps the box in front of her on the table and takes a long drink. "That. I. Have."

"Soooo," I say. "What's this?" I gesture toward the box that she obviously wants me to notice.

"It's your grandmother," she says.

"What?" I'm suddenly freezing underneath all my layers of yarn.

"Her cremains," my mom clarifies. "They were delivered this afternoon. With a letter." She laughs again. "More instructions from beyond the grave."

"Instructions?"

My mom pulls a folded letter out of her pocket and hands it to me. My hands shake as I open it and read some of my grandmother's last words.

"Oh my God," I say, which makes my mom laugh and laugh. "Is this for real? Are you serious?"

"It is!" she says, sounding gleeful. "And I am, Sulie. I am very, very serious."

"Wow."

My mom's laughter turns into a sudden fit of sobbing.

"I can't do it," she says. "I can't. I'm the worst daughter ever because I just can't honor my mother's last wishes." She looks up at me, desperate, pleading for me to absolve her in some way. "I'm not like you or your grandmother. I want things to be neat and orderly. Funerals should be somber, and ashes should be placed in decorative urns and forgotten about. I want life to be quiet and easy. I hate messes! Do you know, out of all the things to hate in the world, like poverty and disease and corruption and out-of-control viruses, I think I hate messes the most?" She's laughing again, rocking back and forth in her chair. I'm afraid she's going to knock over her glass. "And this is gonna be messy, Sulie. It's gonna be so, so messy. And sad, Sulie." Her voice catches. She look at me, straight-faced again and says, "It's gonna be so, so sad."

"It's what Grandma wanted," I say.

"No," my mom says. She holds up a finger, telling me to wait while she drains her wine glass. "My mother did not want us to be sad."

"So what are you going to do?" I hold the letter outlining my grandmother's plan out to my mom.

"I don't know," my mother says sadly, making no move to reclaim Grandma's instructions. "I can't even bring myself to open this box."

I look at my mother, who's never seemed so pathetic, and try to remember that she is grieving, that—even though she and her mother always seemed to be at odds—she must be just as sad as I am that Grandma is no longer with us. I look at the box, and I pull my scarf a little tighter around my neck and say, "I'll do it. I'll fulfill Grandma's Nell's last wishes."

My mother looks up at me, her eyes wide and childlike. "Really?" she asks like a little girl. "Sulie? For real? Are you sure?"

"Yeah," I say. "I'm sure."

My mother gets up, her face full of relief and gratitude, and leans in for a hug. I stiffen as she reaches for me but manage to get a hand on her back and give her a cursory, probably not-comforting-at-all pat or two before she lets go.

"Thank you," she says. "I know your grandma would be so proud of you."

My mom sighs and heads off to her room, and I'm left there alone in the kitchen with a letter I keep hoping is some kind of a joke and a box that, supposedly, among other things, contains what's left of my grandmother. I, too, can't seem to make myself open the box, so I take it to my room and put it on my dresser, where I feel it watching me all night while I bury myself in a den of crochet.

Cam is busy twirling Mia around for sold-out crowds all day on Saturday, so I'm on my own. I can't hang out in the main part of the house because my mom's puttering around, cleaning and decorating her new guest room, a.k.a. the place where Grandma died. I'd like to bet her a million dollars nobody ever sleeps in there again, but she's bought new sheets and a boring white comforter and changed out the curtains, and she thinks that those things will make it not be Grandma's room anymore. I also can't just stay in my room because I'm very aware of the unopened box of Grandma's ashes staring me in the face, so I decide to go out. But I feel bad leaving Grandma behind—nobody loved an outing like Grandma Nell did—so I shove the cardboard box into the oversized sunflower bag Brandi so recently returned to me and take her along for the ride. She's heavy, but the weight is comforting somehow.

I pretend I don't know where I'm going. But I do. I know.

I park on the street and approach on foot. I find the building I'm looking for and cross the street, unable to make myself go in. I camp out at a bus stop shelter and just stare at the plain, gray façade of Mission Possible.

I watch people go in and out. Some of them are obviously homeless, others…I'm not so sure. They wear khaki pants and dress shoes with scruffy-looking coats. I wonder whether some of these almost-but-not-quite-put-together people are in transition, are just starting to get back to work and back to life indoors.

It's cold out, but I've got three sweaters, two scarves, and a hat on, so I sit at the bus stop for a long time. Grandma sits with me in companionable silence, in her unopened cardboard box inside her old handbag, and I'd like to think she's enjoying being out in the city and doing some people-watching with me.

Eventually, Brandi leaves Mission Possible and steps out onto the sidewalk. I recognize her right away. She's tall and not overweight, but bulky, like maybe she works out a lot, and her springy hair sticks out from under a blue knit cap. She's wearing ear buds, walking like she's stepping in time to some upbeat music. She starts walking down the street, and I follow, bumping into a few people and a sign post as I try to watch her across four lanes of traffic. I lose her when she disappears into the yawning mouth of a parking garage. By the time I cross the street, she's been swallowed whole, no sign of her anywhere.

I do the same thing on Sunday—loiter outside Brandi's workplace, watching people come and go. I've parked in the garage I saw Brandi walk into on Saturday, so I think this time I have a chance of following her to her car and tracking her home. I have a strange desire to see where she lives. I'm both intrigued by Brandi's obvious strength and sense of purpose and terrified of her boldness. I tell myself I'm working up the nerve to ask her about volunteering at the mission, that anyone would take their time and scope out the situation before approaching her.

During what must be her lunch break, Brandi emerges from the plain, gray building again, and I'm determined to see where she goes to eat. I think that maybe, after she's done, I'll order the same thing she did and, in that way, forge a connection with her. Grandma weighs me down a bit, her weight tugging at my shoulder as I sneak along the sidewalk, half a block behind Brandi.

At an intersection, Brandi rounds on her heel and shouts, "Hey!"

I'm not stealthy by nature, and this is my first stalking, so I have no idea what to do. I duck into a nearby doorway. I'm breathing hard and feeling my heart hammer and thinking I might be in the clear when Brandi fills up the entire doorway, casting a shadow over me and Grandma.

"Hey, Sunflower Bag. You ever gonna talk to me? Or just follow me around forever?"

"Um. Talk?"

"Right. So talk."

"Um. Now?"

Brandi reaches out and touches the sunflower-print purse hanging at my side. "You're using it," she says. "Your grandma's bag."

"Yeah," I say. "I mean, I set it free, and it came back to me, so it's mine, right? Isn't there some saying about that?" I feel like it would be weird to tell her that, actually, Grandma Nell is using the purse right now.

"I guess." Brandi narrows her eyes at me. "It's not a really great bag to bring when you're stalking people, though. I mean, it's bright. I saw it coming from a mile away yesterday. If I hadn't known you were kind to my mom at the end of her life, I might have called the cops by now."

I blush and look down at my feet.

"So," Brandi says, taking up an awful lot of room in the doorway. "What do you want to talk about?"

I swallow and unwrap and rewrap one of my scarves. "Um, the mission? Maybe helping out at the mission?"

Brandi steps back, and I feel a little less claustrophobic. She nods and smiles a little. "All right," she says. "You wanna grab some lunch?"

"Yeah," I say. "Lunch would be great."

We go to this little sub shop on the next block and order a couple of turkey sandwiches and cups of what Brandi promises me is the best cheddar-broccoli soup in town. As soon as I take a taste, I think she's probably right.

We sit next to the window. I feel too shy to look at Brandi the whole time, so I do a lot of people-watching. Everyone is hurrying past me with somewhere to be, and Brandi has to be back at work in an hour. I'm the only person in the world who's doing nothing right now. Me, and Grandma Nell, who's still stuck inside a box inside my bag. When Brandi asks me why I want to work at the mission, that's pretty much what I tell her. That I want to do more in the world, and she nods, says she gets it.

"This is not a hobby, though," she says. "Or something you can do once in a while when you're bored. Working to help these people change their lives requires a certain level of commitment."

I take a bite of my sub, so I won't have to say anything back, but I nod with what I hope looks like enthusiasm.

"So, why the homeless?" Brandi asks. "I mean, there are lots of places to volunteer in the city, plenty of places closer to your house, even. Tons of causes. Why do you care about getting people off the streets?"

I take another deliberate bite of my sandwich and take my time chewing, but I know this question requires an actual verbal response.

"Well," I say, swallowing. "OK. Before my friend Cam thought of the blessing bag idea? My mom was going to just donate all of my grandmother's stuff to this church thrift shop.

Which was for a good cause and everything, right? But, I mean, we were just going to toss it all into these big collection bins and then some worker who drew the short straw the next day was going to unload it all and sort it and *appraise* it and put a price tag on it. Then, some old lady or other would have come into the shop and bought it and maybe liked it or used it for a little while and then left it in the back of her closet, forgotten, until *she* died and *her* daughter and granddaughter had to come and clean it out and put it right back into the same donation bin…"

I know I'm rambling, but Brandi's really listening to me, and it feels good to talk, so I keep going.

"…so, like, all Grandma's stuff would have just gone through this whole cycle of…I dunno…consumerism, and I hated that thought. Couldn't stand it. But when we handed the bags and shawls and hats out to people on the street, they really *appreciated* them, you know. They didn't use them to fill up their already overstuffed closets; they wore my grandma's handmade sweaters and scarves for warmth, right then, in the moment. They needed them. And for most of them, I could see that it hurt their pride to take the handout, to take what they needed from people who wanted to give it to them. Which sucks. And I thought it shouldn't have to be like that, you know? And I saw gratitude too. For such a small, small thing. Real gratitude, from people like your mom, who hugged me and my friend half to death and reminded us both how beautiful life is—" Brandi's eyes are brimming with tears, so I stop. "I'm sorry," I say. "Oh my God, I'm so sorry."

"No," Brandi says, sitting up straighter and blinking fast. "Don't be. That's, like, the best reason I ever heard of for some-one wanting to work at the mission."

While we finish lunch, Brandi tells me about some of the work Mission Possible does for its clients, people they select from a pool of applicants based on, among other things, their apparent work ethic. They help their clients find clothes they can wear to interviews and workplaces, assist them with temporary housing, and help them with things like opening bank accounts and establishing some kind of credit.

"It's about more than finding someone a fast-food job that doesn't pay the rent, so they wind up back out on the streets in a few months," she says. "Like you said, it's giving people their pride back. Helping them find a way to earn what they need not just to get through the day but for the foreseeable future. So they don't have to feel like they're getting a handout ever again."

Brandi tells me she works one-on-one with her clients and that her job is really rewarding. She and her coworkers do everything from tutoring to style consulting to interview prep to paperwork for government assistance. She says when she sees someone she's been working with long-term really come into their own, it feels amazing. "This job can be heartbreaking, though too," she warns me. "Not every person who walks through the front door of Mission Possible leaves as a success story."

Brandi has to get back to work, and I offer to walk her back to the mission. Brandi expertly dodges pedestrians, bypasses a group of tourists on Segways, and jaywalks across a major intersection as I hurry to keep up. As we walk, she tells me she's working toward a degree in social work at the University of North Carolina in Charlotte. I tell her that sounds really cool, and she asks what my plans are for next year.

"Um, undecided?" I tell her. "I'm not really the best at planning."

Brandi gives me a skeptical look. A car horn blares as she steps off the sidewalk into traffic, but she ignores it, so I do too and follow her into the crosswalk.

"I was just starting to think about next year when my grandmother got really sick," I tell her a little breathlessly. "I knew I didn't want to leave here, you know, because my mom and my best friend are here and, back then, so was my Grandma…so I was thinking about maybe applying to college close to home, but I haven't really gotten around to applying anywhere. Seeing what my grandmother went through made me think I should do something with the elderly, you know? Not in healthcare, necessarily, but maybe art therapy? Or work at a senior center? So more people like my grandma could get out and about and have some different experiences at the ends of their lives?"

Brandi nods. "Those all sound like good plans to me," she says. "And, at Mission Possible, a lot of our clients are older people, so that could be good experience for you." She offers to hook me up with some information about the UNC School of Social Work, and I tell her I'd really appreciate that.

"I'm sorry for stalking you all weekend," I say when we get back to her building.

"No sweat," she tells me with a smile. "I'm glad you did."

As I drive home, my phone dings a few times, and I assume it's Cam, but when I reach my driveway, I'm surprised to see that Brandi has sent me a bunch of links to her undergraduate program in the city. The last message reads, "Application deadlines are coming up fast!!!" I grab Grandma off the passenger seat and carry her into the house.

Chapter Twelve

Monday is the first day of finals. I don't know how I don't know about this. Where did the semester go? And how could none of my teachers have mentioned this even once over the course of the last couple weeks? They must really be falling down on the job.

"Finals!" I say to Cam in the chaos of the senior hallway. He steers me away from my usual homeroom and leads me toward my first scheduled exam instead. "Did you know about this?"

"Yes?" he says, exasperated. "Why do you think I've been studying until midnight for the past two weeks?" Cam is graduating early and plans to walk in the winter commencement ceremony in January. These are his last exams ever. I guess maybe he did mention something about that a while back…

The good news is that final-exam days are half days. The bad news is that even if I'd had a whole week to spend on one exam booklet, I'd never get higher than a C at this point.

When the bell rings, Cam looks really concerned. "Listen," he says. "Come over later. I'll help you cram for tomorrow."

"Forget it," I say. "You said you already studied."

"I could use a refresher," he says, but I know he's lying.

"You have enough stress in your life right now. Don't worry about my exams. I'll be fine."

Cam shoots me a serious face. "Come over," he says. "I just have to hit the gym first. Give me, like, an hour."

"The gym?"

"No rehearsal today. Our one day off before the final push leading up to Senior Showcase. May as well work out."

"Ever heard of resting?" I ask him.

Cam grins. "Nope."

I know his workout will last more than an hour, so I wait two before I knock on Cam's front door.

"He's in the tub," Mom Rachel tells me, disgusted. "Ice bath. He went to the gym today. Can you believe that? On his one day off! Go see if you can talk some sense into him, will you, Sulie?"

"Sure," I say. "I'll try."

The bathroom door is open, but I knock anyway. "Are you decent?" I say, so he'll know it's me.

"Decent," he says, "but somewhat hypothermic. Come on in."

Cam's waist-deep in a tub of ice water, wearing spandex shorts and a bulky sweatshirt. An empty twenty-pound ice bag sits in a puddle on the floor. Cam's phone is acting as a timer. He's set it for fifteen minutes. He still has eight minutes left in the ice.

"You're a nut job, you know that?" I say, sitting on the edge of the tub. "Mom Rachel seems kind of worried about you."

"I'm fine," he says. He tries to smile, but his lips are trembling.

"No, you're not," I tell him. I take off the crocheted hat I'm wearing and shove it on his head. I unwrap one of my scarves and coil it around his neck.

"Thanks," he says, and I can hear his teeth chattering.

"You should have just taken the day off today," I tell him.

"I couldn't, OK?" he snaps. "God. I wish everyone would stop saying stuff like that to me! I have Senior Showcase this weekend and my audition the following week! Now is not the time to be taking days off!"

"Cam," I say, trying to sound calm and reasonable. "You've got your showcase routines down cold. And I thought this audition was just a formality."

"My showcase stuff has been on the back burner too long thanks to *The Nutcracker*. All the passion's gone out of it. And the Queen City audition isn't a formality. Renee says she's sure they'll take me because of her connections there, but I still have to show up and make the cut. It's a real dance company, Sulie! A serious job! The start of my whole career! If I blow it, all of next year goes down the drain. Everything I've worked for will be gone!"

He's really shivering now, so I grab a towel off a nearby rack and wrap it around his shoulders and rub his back. I think about all the assholes at our school who spent so many years picking on Cam for not being tough enough, calling him a sissy and a wimp. I wish they could see him right now. I wonder how many varsity football or basketball players spent our half day of freedom at the gym or soaking their muscles in an ice bath. I'm betting zero. Traditionally, the cool jocks all go to the movies and out for burgers with their push-up-bra-wearing girlfriends after exams. Cam probably could have gone with them. I'm sure he was invited, even. But he chose this. Cam always chooses this.

Finally, the timer beeps, and I pull the plug on the ice bath, pain exploding in my hand as I plunge it into the freezing water. Cam's feet have gone numb, so I hold on to him as he stands up, and he lets me help him step out of the tub. I toss my stuff on his bed and go make him a cup of green tea while he towels off and throws on two layers of dry sweats and some thick woolen socks. He keeps wearing my hat and scarf, and I let him.

When I bring him his tea, Cam's sitting in bed, huddled underneath his comforter. I grab a fleece blanket off the foot of the bed and drape that over him as well. It always takes him a while to warm back up, but he says that's part of the process. It's all supposed to be very good for his muscles. His hands are still shaking as I hand him his steaming mug.

"Thanks," he says and takes a careful sip and wrinkles up his nose. Cam hates the taste of green tea, but he thinks it's good for him.

"No problem," I say. I sit next to him, on top of all his covers.

"So, what's this?" he asks me, nudging the sunflower bag I'd tossed onto his bed. He's scooted it over next to the wall and climbed into bed right beside it. "Wasn't that your grandma's bag?"

"It was," I say. "Um, actually? It kind of still is." I tell him what's inside. I can see that his gut reaction is that he wants my dead grandmother out of his bed right away, so I grab the purse by its shaggy handle and set it on the floor. "Sorry," I say. "I've been carrying her around for days now, and I guess I'm just used to it."

Cam stares at me. He just spent a quarter of an hour half-submerged in ice, and, somehow, I'm the craziest person in the room.

I take a deep breath and tell him about Grandma's letter.

Cam's face lights up with one of his huge smiles. "I love it!" he says. "Oh, Grandma Nell! This is awesome!"

"What it is is a mess," I tell him. "And I told my mom I'd take care of it, so it's my mess, but I haven't even had the courage to open up the box yet."

"So open it."

"Right now?"

"Why not?"

"I dunno." I look around his room, trying to find a suitable place to deal with Grandma's cremains.

"Would you rather be alone?" Cam asks.

"No."

"Good." Cam reaches across me to set his mug on the nightstand and leans over the edge of the bed to grab the sunflower bag. He drops it into my lap. "Go for it," he says.

I pull out the box and balance it on my thighs.

"Wait," Cam says. "She's, like, *in* something, right?"

"Yes," I say. "I think so. She paid for some kind of a temporary urn."

"Right."

We press our sides together, leaning over the box, and I open the tape that's sealing it shut and pull back the cardboard flaps. Nothing at all happens, and Cam and I both laugh nervously, like maybe we expected Grandma's ghost to jump out at us or something.

Grandma's temporary "urn" is a plain black plastic box. With trembling fingers, I lift the lid. Inside is a plastic bag full of what must be her ashes. The bag is tied shut with a plain old twist tie, like the kind you find on a loaf of bread, and that strikes me as completely ridiculous. I start laughing. And also crying a little.

Cam puts one hand on my shoulder and reaches into the box with the other. He pulls out a fistful of plastic rainbow-striped loot bags, the kind they sell for little-kid birthday parties, and holds them up for me to see. I take them from him and shake my head, laughing again.

"Sulie!" Cam says, pulling a piece of paper out of the box. "It's a sign!" He holds up the Senior Stars meeting calendar my grandmother had enclosed. "There's a meeting in two hours!"

I take the sheet from him and study it. It's definitely a sign all right. A sign that I won't be studying for finals tonight after all.

"Let's work at the kitchen table," Cam says, crawling out from under the covers. "No offense, but if we spill in here, I'll never sleep again."

Chapter Thirteen

If Mom Rachel objects to us sorting out her late neighbor's cremains in the middle of her kitchen table, she keeps it to herself. Mom Kelly is still at work, and what she doesn't know won't hurt her.

Grandma really has thought of everything: the Senior Stars meeting schedule, the names and addresses of a couple local businesses, a list of her nearest and dearest, a Sharpie marker, and, of course, a bunch of shiny gold twist-ties.

"How about I label the bags and you fill them?" Cam says.

We both stare at the bag full of what used to be my beloved Grandma Nell.

"Or I could label the bags," I offer. "And you could scoop the ashes."

We stare at the cremains some more.

"We'll take turns," Cam says grimly, rolling up his sleeves.

"I love you, you know that?" I tell him, starting to choke up.

"I love you too," he says and smiles. "But don't go to pieces on me right now, OK, Su-Su? We need to focus here. That meeting is starting soon, and these ashes aren't going to divvy themselves up."

"Right." I clear my throat and blink. I can do this. We can do this.

We label the rainbow party favor bags with the names of my grandma's closest friends and relatives, and then, into each little bag, we dump two heaping plastic spoonfuls of her remains. We tie the bags off with the shiny ties Grandma provided and pile them in her big, bright sunflower handbag. There's just enough of Grandma Nell to go around, and I wonder how she could possibly have planned that.

"There's one in here for you," I say to Cam.

"I know," he says. "I can't believe it! I'm honored, really. I already know what I want to do with her!"

"Lucky you," I mutter as Cam disappears into his room to take off all his sweats before we leave for the Stars' meeting.

I feel really nervous on the ride to the community center where the Senior Stars meet. I tug on my huge crocheted cardigan, wishing I could just disappear inside of it. Cam's given me back my hat and scarf, so I have plenty of neckwear on too, but all the scarves in the world won't cover up the huge lump forming in my throat.

The Senior Stars seem really happy to see us when we walk into the Community Room at the senior center. The plain, institutional-looking room with white-tiled floors and terrible fluorescent lighting is used for all kinds of events, but the Stars make it their own for their meetings, draping glittery star-covered tablecloths over everything, tacking shiny star garlands over the windows and hanging big plastic stars from the panels of the drop ceiling. It feels a little bit like we've just walked into a theme party.

"Sulie!" May says. "And the sweet and handsome Camden!" She hugs us both and actually pinches Cam's cheek.

Addie takes things a step further and slaps him playfully on the ass as she says her hellos. Cam is blushing, but I can tell he loves all the old-lady attention.

"Look who it is!" another lady whose name I've forgotten exclaims. She grabs my upper arms and looks me right in the eye, super serious-like. "Do you know…? I could have sworn I saw your grandmother in Uptown the other day. I went in to lunch with a friend and, lo and behold, around the corner comes a woman wearing a shawl that looked exactly like something your grandmother would have made. She had a very Nell-ish hat and handbag too." She sighs. "When she got closer, of course, I could see that it definitely wasn't her, but it was a sign. It was a sign, I think." She nods sagely. "It was definitely a sign."

"A sign that our blessing bags are being put to good use," Cam whispers after she walks away. It's all I can do to keep from laughing, which is a nice distraction from the ball of nerves that's still bouncing up and down in my stomach.

The woman I recognize as the belly dancer from Grandma's funeral approaches us. "I wondered when we'd be seeing you," she says to me with a wink.

I'm a little relieved to think that maybe Grandma's last wishes won't be a complete shock to everyone in the room at least. The woman insists we take some punch and cookies from the buffet they have set up along one wall. I'm not sure, but I think the punch has been spiked. I drain my whole cup and imagine it gives me courage.

"All right, all right. Listen up!" my grandma's friend Theresa, the one who told us the Nashville story at Tony Baloney's, says as she calls the meeting to order. "We have some special guests with us this evening: Nell Foster's granddaughter, Sulie, and her friend Camden. They have a favor they'd like to ask of us on Nell's behalf, so turn up your damn hearing aids and pay attention!"

I stand up, clutching the big sunflower purse full of party bags, and clear my throat. "I'd like to read you a letter from my grandmother," I say. "'Dear Loved Ones...'" My voice trembles, but I think the old ladies can all hear me. "'I am writing to you from beyond the grave to ask for your help scattering my remains. Please accept a small portion of my ashes and do with them what you will. Now, if you made the list, you're definitely creative enough to come up with a final resting place for me that's far more exciting than your fireplace mantle or some old cemetery. Scatter me somewhere we shared a memory, somewhere you love that I never got to experience, or somewhere that will make you laugh when you think back on it. Thank you, and I love you. Nell.'"

I'm sniffling and tugging uncomfortably at my big sweater, and Cam stands up next to me and puts a hand on my shoulder.

"I know this is kind of weird," I say, trying my best to smile out at the Senior Stars, some of whom are crying now. "But will you guys do it?"

"Damn skippy we will!" someone yells out, and everyone else applauds.

"OK," I say, reaching into Grandma's big sunflower purse and pulling out the first party bag. "Geraldine Watson?"

"Here!" Geraldine jumps up and waves her arms in the air like she just won at bingo. Cam takes her bag of ashes from me and hands it to her.

"Adeline Pierce?"

"That's me!" Addie comes forward to claim her prize.

"Sallie Vincent?"

One by one, the Senior Stars take their little pieces of Grandma. They all ooh and ahh over the adorable bags and talk excitedly about what they're going to do with my grandmother.

"I'm taking her to the beach this summer," one lady says. "Myrtle Beach, I think. Remember that time we all tried parasailing there? I think I'm gonna go up in one of those parasails and let Nellie fly out over the water!"

"It's Nashville for me," Addie says. She starts laughing, remembering the band tour bus mix-up or some other funny story. "That was one hell of a good time."

"Atlantic City!"

"The mountains!"

"The lake!"

"Paris! Remember how we always talked about going to Paris someday? Well, life's short. I'm gonna do it. Booking my flight tonight! And I'm gonna take Nellie with me."

Every single one of Grandma's friends insists on hugging us before we go, and I worry that I'm going to be fatally overcome by the smell of old-lady perfume and hairspray or jabbed to death with bony elbows, but I hug them all back anyway, because, apparently, not one of them thinks that receiving a plastic loot bag full of the cremains of one of their members is even a tiny bit weird. And I really, really appreciate that.

They want us to stay and have more punch and cookies, but we tell them we have a few more stops to make, and they understand completely.

We go over to Tony Baloney's. Tony and his assistant are being slammed with a dinner rush, and Cam suddenly realizes he's starving, so we order a couple of pastrami sandwiches and sit down to wait for a lull. When there's no line at the counter, we approach Tony and introduce ourselves.

"Of course!" Tony says. "I remember you. That was some after-funeral party, huh?" Tony smiles. "Your grandmother was really something else."

"She was," I tell him, handing over Grandma's letter for him to look at. "She definitely was."

Tony reads the letter and blinks his eyes a lot and looks kind of nervous as we hand a plastic baggie of human remains across his deli counter.

"Um, I'm not so sure about having them in the restaurant," he says, "but I'd love to put her in the flower boxes out front. Let her greet her old friends when they come for lunch."

"I think she would love that," I tell him.

Tony sniffles. "She was a great lady," he says. "Really special. She always made time to talk to this schmuck of a deli guy whenever she came in to eat."

Cam leans across the counter and offers Tony a hug, and Tony accepts it. He's smiling and shaking his head at his bag of ashes when we leave.

"The jazz club?" Cam asks as we get back into his car.

"May as well," I say. "I hope Gordo is there."

It turns out that Gordo is always there, at least according to the hostess. He pretty much has his own bar stool, and he plays saxophone every single night. I recognize him right away, and we introduce ourselves, telling him how much we enjoyed his playing at Grandma's funeral.

"Shoot," he says. "That was one heck of a send-off for Miss Nellie."

"And it's not quite over yet," I tell him. I give him Grandma's message and his loot bag full of ashes.

"Ah!" he smiles and clutches the party bag to his heart. "I know just where I'm going to put her. I have the perfect spot." He doesn't elaborate, and we don't ask him to.

A man in a snazzy-looking suit with no tie and a pair of dark sunglasses taps Gordo on the shoulder. "Hey, man. You ready? You promised me one song before I have to go."

"Frankie, you blind sonofabitch." Gordo claps the man on the back. "How do you always find me?"

Frankie smiles. "You always sit right here, you big dummy. It's not like you're hidin'. I just follow the smell."

The two men laugh.

"I've got company," Gordo tells his friend. "Nellie's grand-daughter and her boyfriend."

"He's not my—" I start, but Frankie doesn't care who's going out with whom.

"Good," he says. "More people to hear me sing. Now, come on, man. I'm not gettin' any younger, you hear?"

"Duty calls," Gordo says to us. He places Grandma's ashes carefully in his breast pocket. "Thanks for coming by," he says. "You should stay for a while. Hang out and enjoy the show. Chelsea!" He signals to the woman behind the bar. "Get a couple drinks for my friends here and put them on my tab."

Chelsea rolls her eyes. "Your tab's as long as my bar, Gordo." She's smiling, though. "You'd better make this a really good set."

Gordo smiles and takes a funny little goodbye bow. "That's

my cue," he says, his eyes twinkling. He puts a hand under Frankie's elbow and leads him to the stage.

I hop up onto his bar stool, and Cam takes the one next to it. Chelsea asks us what we'd like to drink, and we both order a Coke. I look around and notice we're the only people in the place under thirty. I run my hand along the edge of the bar. I'd never even heard of this jazz club until I read my grandma's last wishes. Did she come here often to hear Gordo play? Did she sit right here on this stool, even, leaning up against this bar, laughing and chatting and ordering drinks from Chelsea? She must have; she knew Gordo's schedule well enough to write it down. I let myself pretend for just a second that she is sitting here with me, smiling in anticipation of Gordo's music.

Frankie steps up to the microphone and Gordo grabs his sax. A piano player and a drummer take the stage as well. They start to play, and, as Frankie's smooth voice wraps itself around the first line of "The Dock of the Bay," the whole club starts to cheer. I've heard this song a million times, in every elevator in the greater Charlotte area, but there's something really magical happening in the jazz club right now, and everybody knows it. Frankie's singing with so much feeling, and Gordo's saxophone is like a whole other kind of voice, and everybody's grooving in their seats. A few people even stand up and sway back and forth. Cam's bopping up and down in time to the music, and even I'm involuntarily nodding along.

Frankie's voice transports me to that bay. I'm sitting there on the dock with him, waiting and waiting for absolutely nothing and watching the ships and the tides come and go. It's amazing. I wish my grandmother had heard it. I wonder whether she did hear it, think that maybe she came here to listen to Gordo's sax all the time, and I never even knew it.

"I'm not crying," I say when I feel Cam put his hand on my back.

"OK."

We stay for a few more songs and then decide we have to get going. We wave goodbye to Gordo between numbers, and he puts his hand over his heart, over the bag full of Grandma Nell, in farewell.

"Can we make one more stop?" Cam asks as we wait for his car to warm up.

"Sure," I say.

I'm not really surprised when Cam drives to the park we used to play at as little kids and stops. I pull my cardigan tight to keep a sob from escaping.

"I want to put Grandma Nell here," Cam says. "In the duck pond."

"That's perfect," I tell him, and we get out of the car.

We hold hands as we walk across the dark park toward the water. We stand at the edge, gazing out at the black ripples as if they were part of an endless sea instead of some glorified puddle whose other shore we can plainly see in the moonlight.

"Your grandma used to take us here almost every day when we were little," Cam says.

"I know."

"All the other moms and grandmas sat on benches, but not her. She ran around with us and took us on little nature walks and ate picnic lunches sitting on the ground."

"I know."

"And she always let us feed the ducks."

"I know, Cam." I don't think I can survive this much longer. I wish he'd dump his ashes and move on already.

"Remember that time I fell in the pond?" Cam laughs, his eyes bright with moonlight. "She told me not to go too close to the edge, but I did anyway, and I tripped and fell in, and I was soaked from head to toe, and my clothes were full of brown, rotten pond scum, but Grandma Nell didn't yell at me or anything. She didn't even rat me out to my moms. She just laughed and took me home and cleaned me up and washed my clothes in your machine and gave us some of her Sunday cakes to eat while they dried."

"I remember, Cam, OK?"

Cam smiles at me a little sadly and squeezes my hand. Then, he lets go of me and reaches into the sunflower purse for his bag of ashes. He goes too close to the edge to dump them into the water, and I half expect him to fall in. I'm almost disappointed that he doesn't. When he comes back to stand next to me again, tears are streaming down his face.

"Stop it," I say. "Or I'm gonna cry too."

"You are crying," he says, and I realize he's right.

"I think I need a hug," I tell him.

"Me too," he says, and we hold on to each other for dear life.

When we get back to my house, I'm all cried out and "The Dock of the Bay" is on repeat in my head.

"Are you OK?" Cam asks me.

"Yeah. You?"

"Yeah." He's smiling again. "Have you decided what you want to do with your portion of the ashes?"

I shake my head.

"Well, let me know if you need any help, you know, setting them free or whatever."

"OK."

"You want me to hang out a while and help you study for tomorrow?"

"Nah." It's late, and I'm beat, and I know Cam must be exhausted too. He spent what was left of his one day to relax helping me run the weirdest, most emotionally taxing errands ever.

"Sulie. You have to study."

"I did," I tell him. "I studied while you were at the gym."

"Really?"

"Yeah."

No. I didn't. Not really. I spent the whole time drawing Brandi, trying to get just the right mix of ferocity and anger and kindness into her eyes.

"I'll see you tomorrow, OK?" I say.

"OK," Cam says. "I have my regular dance classes plus extra rehearsals all week again, but I'll catch you at school."

"I understand. And thanks for tonight. I couldn't have done this without you."

Cam grins. "I feel like I should be thanking you. And Grandma Nell. Tonight was actually a really great night."

I smile too. "Yeah," I say. "I guess it was."

When I get inside, my mom's on the couch watching TV. There's no wine glass in sight, which means either she's in a better mood today or she's already stinking drunk.

"Here," I say and toss her a party bag full of her mother.

"Is this...?"

"It is."

"So...you did it, then?" she asks, staring at the rainbow-printed bag in her lap.

"Yup. Cam helped."

"How was it?"

I think about that for a second. "Messy," I say. "But good messy." I actually feel sorry for my mother for being left out of the whole thing. She didn't get to drink punch with the Stars or find out that Grandma will be fertilizing Tony's flowers or hear the best rendition of "The Dock of the Bay" ever performed in the history of the world. She missed everything. "What are you going to do with your ashes?" I ask her.

"I don't know," she says, bewildered. She shakes her head and finally tears her eyes away from her mom's cremains to look at me. "I'm sort of surprised I made the list."

"I'm not," I say, and I think I see tears welling in my mother's eyes. I've already cried enough for one day, so I turn away from her. "Well, goodnight," I call over my shoulder.

I go to my room, but I don't sleep. There's too much to draw: excited old ladies and a sad deli schmuck and a saxophone player with a secret in his pocket and a blind man who paints pictures with his voice.

Chapter Fourteen

My second day of exams goes about as well as my first. "How'd you do?" Cam asks me when the last one is finished for the day.

"Great. Aced it. For sure."

"What did you put for number ten? The strongest type of chemical bond in a biological system?"

"Um. Forty-two. You?"

"Shit, Sulie." Cam stops walking. "That's it," he says. "I'm taking you home right now, and we're going to study for tomorrow."

"You have rehearsal."

"I don't care."

"I do. I've got this, OK? I was just messing with you. I killed those tests this morning. Honest." I give Cam my most earnest face, my mouth a straight, serious line, my eyebrows pulling together just a little, my head tilted slightly to one side.

"Really?" He sounds skeptical.

"Yes! And I'm on my way to the guidance office right now for some academic advising, so don't make me late."

"Stop it."

"You don't believe me?"

"Nope."

"Fine. Walk with me."

So he does.

"Hi," I say to the woman at the desk when we get there. "Sulie Bingle? I have an appointment." I sneak a peek at my phone, do a quick web search for "strongest chemical bond biology."

"Yes, Miss Bingle. It'll be just a minute. Have a seat."

I give Cam a triumphant look and plop down into a vinyl-covered chair.

"Sorry," he says.

"No problem," I tell him.

"I've just been worried about you."

"Well, don't be. And don't miss rehearsal on my account. Mia's not gonna lift and twirl herself in the showcase on Saturday night, right?"

Cam still looks uncertain.

"Covalent," I tell him, sounding as exasperated as possible. "A covalent bond is the strongest type of chemical bond in a biological system."

Cam finally cracks a smile. "All right," he says. "I'm going."

I don't really get any academic advice. I just request a copy of my transcript. I think it's best to get one now before my final-exam grades are in for the semester.

I spend the rest of the half day filling out an online UNC application and then burying myself in my sketchbook. I text Brandi to let her know I'm applying to her program, and she actually calls me and says she talked to her boss. They're willing to train me as an intern if I'm still interested in working at the mission. She says it could turn into a paid position for the summer and maybe even extend into next school year.

"We're a nonprofit," she says, "so the pay's not much. But you get a lot more out of it than just money."

I tell her that sounds good. I think back to the night of the blessing bags and smile just a little. If working at the mission is anything like passing out those bags, I think it will be a lot better than good.

She wants to know if I have any free time this week to come for an orientation.

I tell her I have exams this week, so, yeah. I have loads of free time.

I spend an entire afternoon at Mission Possible, getting oriented. I learn how to file papers and sort clothing donations and answer phones. I don't single-handedly rescue even one person from life on the streets, and it's kind of a letdown. Brandi can tell, I think, because she makes a big deal about how answering even one phone call makes a small difference and how lots of small differences add up to really big, important differences. She says that, if I want to, I can work with her all day on Saturday, and I tell her, yeah, I'd love to.

I'm kind of nervous for my first full day at the mission, so I wear this cozy crocheted sweater that's longer in the back than it is in the front. It fits snugly, and I imagine Grandma Nell is giving me a little squeeze of encouragement. For good measure, I tie on two scarves, but no more, because I don't want to, like, rub it in the homeless people's faces that I have access to a whole pile of handmade winter wear and they don't.

The first thing that happens as I settle in to shadow Brandi is that a prospective client tries to steal my wallet right out of

Grandma's happy yellow sunflower purse. Brandi catches him in the act, rolls her eyes, sends the thief back out onto the streets, and suggests I keep my bag in one of the staff lockers for the rest of the day. I decide to do what she says because the wallet is one thing, but I still have my party bag full of Grandma Nell in my purse, and if one of the mission's clients were to steal it, I would lose what's left of my mind.

The second thing that happens is that another prospective client throws up on my jeans. Brandi helps me clean up as best I can, but I'm really, really bad with barf, so I excuse myself and go root through my car to find something else to put on. All I can come up with is a pair of black knit dance pants with a bright-red stripe down one leg and a funny logo on the hip that Cam left behind in my trunk after one of his ballet classes. They stopped at his calves, but they're longer and baggier on me and look fairly ridiculous, so I go back to work worried that I both smell and look like a prospective client myself.

The third thing that happens is that I meet Sarah. She's an elementary school teacher from the Midwest who moved here to care for her sick mother. When her mom died, she didn't go back to work because she sank into a deep depression. Between her mother's medical bills and her own living expenses, she soon blew through her modest savings account and was genuinely surprised to find herself out on the streets. Now, Mission Possible is trying to help her get a teaching position again. She'll need to update her license and explain away the fact that she got fired from her last job for not showing up, but Brandi's helped her line up an interview for a part-time classroom assistant on Monday.

"It's a foot in the door," Brandi keeps reminding her. "A foot in the door."

I get to help Sarah pick an interview outfit from the mission's stockpile of donated dress clothes and go over a bunch of interview prep questions with her. She doesn't have housing ("Yet!" Brandi reminds her), but she has a spot in a good shelter and will be able to get a shower and breakfast before her interview.

"Remember that you don't have to tell them where you live," Brandi says. "You can use Mission Possible as your mailing address if you have to, and make sure you give them your email address. You can come check your mail here anytime, and you still have that emergency cell phone we gave you, so potential employers can contact you that way too."

Sarah nods and seems really nervous. I can tell that she's smart and nice, and I can totally relate to going through a bit of a slump after the loss of a loved one so I really, really hope she gets this job. I shake her hand when she goes to leave and wish her luck. She says it means a lot to her. Her saying that means a lot to me, so I figure we're even.

At the end of the day, Brandi asks me what I thought, whether I'd like to come back. I think about it for a minute. The pickpocket, the barfer. It was like some kind of test. And I passed. I like that. And I like Sarah. I know I didn't really do much for her but cheer her on, but that's something. It's one of Brandi's small differences.

"Yeah," I tell her. "I'll be back."

"What are you doing tonight?" she asks. "You maybe want to run over and take a tour of the UNC campus with me? Get something to eat at SoVi there? The food's surprisingly good."

"I'd actually love that," I say, "but I can't tonight."

"How about tomorrow?" Brandi asks.

"Yeah," I say. "I'm free all day tomorrow. And I'll be wearing my own pants then, soooo…"

"OK," she says, laughing. "We'll do lunch. Tomorrow. In your own pants. I'll call you."

Chapter Fifteen

I'm almost late to Cam's Senior Showcase, which is so not like me that Mom Kelly almost knocks me over when I finally walk through the theater doors.

"Sulie, oh my God," she says, squeezing me so hard that I fear for the integrity of my rib cage. "What happened? We were getting worried!" She's obviously in the throes of one of her preperformance anxiety attacks.

"I'm so sorry," I say. "I was coming from Uptown, and there was just a ton of traffic…"

"It doesn't matter," Mom Rachel says kindly, giving me one of her careful hugs. "We're so glad you made it."

The showcase is being held in a small, experimental theater downstairs from the ballet academy. Unlike *The Nutcracker*, which raises money for charity, there aren't any tickets or assigned seats for the Senior Showcase, and the program is just a photocopied sheet listing the night's performances. There are only eight seniors, so it's not a long list. Everyone is dancing a pas de deux and a solo. The audience is mostly parents and a few invited guests, local friends of Renee's who work in dance or theater. The performance is also being professionally recorded so the kids can use it as a video audition when they apply to colleges or contact dance companies that might not hold auditions in our region.

Cam's not applying to college, but he's nervous anyway because Renee told him some of her friends from the Queen City Company, where she danced professionally before she opened the ballet academy, are coming to watch, and that's the company Cam's auditioning for next week. Obviously, he wants to make a good first impression and has been more on edge than usual about this performance. I glance around, trying to suss out which audience members hold Cam's future in their hands, and peg a group of three people in business attire down front as Renee's Queen City connections. If Mia trips Cam or elbows him in the face in front of these important ballet people, I'll personally break both of her spindly little legs.

Cam's first dance is his pas de deux with Mia. They're dancing to something from Swan Lake, and they both wear these sparkly white and silver costumes. Mia's has feathers all over it. I have to admit, she's so birdlike and light on her feet that she really does look like she could flutter away at any second. And Cam is absolutely princely, of course, strong and precise in his movements. The two of them oversell the romance angle of things, in my honest opinion, but it's an artistic choice, and it's none of my business. At the end of the dance, Mom Kelly is crying, so I know she thinks it was technically excellent. Cam runs off stage, and, for one gleeful minute, I think he's abandoning Mia at last, but he comes right back out a second later with a huge bouquet of roses for her and kisses her on the cheek in front of everyone. She's on Cloud Nine, of course. She really might just fly right off the stage.

There's a female soloist I don't recognize and then Serge dances a perfectly respectable pas de deux with another girl I don't know. I should probably recognize the ballet it's from, but I don't care enough to check my program. Next, James does his solo. It's a beautiful piece set to classical music that incorporates a lot of runs on the piano. James interprets these with lots of jumping and turning in midair to enthusiastic applause. I try to feel a pang of longing, the ache of unrequited love, but I can't. He's still gorgeous, I suppose, but now—at least to me—only in the way you admire from afar. After James, Natalie reprises her Spanish dance solo from *The Nutcracker*, mantilla and all, which I think is pretty lame. What, she couldn't be bothered to learn an extra dance? If I had rotten tomatoes, I'd throw them, but everybody else claps politely, and nobody but me looks like they feel cheated.

For his solo, Cam's dancing as Albrecht from *Giselle*, which he's told me is a super famous role, so he really has to nail it. He does. He crosses the stage with these graceful leaps that make him look like he's flying. Seriously, his hang time is unbelievable. He twists and turns through the air, pirouettes so fast he's basically a blur, and it all looks completely effortless. He uses the whole stage, owns every inch of it, and his excitement has to be felt by everyone in the tiny theater. I know my own heartrate increases with every brilliant step he takes.

Mom Kelly is out-and-out weeping when Cam takes his bow. Mom Rachel whistles, and I'm clapping so hard my hands hurt. Cam looks really happy, and I'm really, really happy for him. All those extra rehearsals, all those extra workouts. The missed social events, the teasing, the ice baths. I can see that it's all been worth it to Cam. There's no way those ballet folks from Queen City didn't just sit up and take notice of him.

Mia flits around on stage in a flouncy little tutu to some fast-paced violin music, and everybody acts like they love it, even though I think at least some of them must be faking. Then, Serge takes the stage alone in nothing but a pair of skin-tight black short shorts. His intensity works much better on stage than it does close-up, commanding his audience's attention. And, for what it's worth, he really is ripped. I glance at my program. I don't recognize the name of the song he's dancing to, and there's a note that says he choreographed the piece himself. I sit up a little straighter in my chair. He looks different than he usually does on stage. His tattoo is clearly visible, and his hair is standing straight up on end. He looks electrified, charged. Serge. Surge.

Serge's music starts, and I'm immediately transported. It's haunting, like it's not even a song, but the ghost of a song, the echo of a feeling felt by a composer eons ago in some parallel universe. When Serge starts to move, he *is* the song. His body and the music are one. He stretches and reaches and lunges. He's powerful, ethereal, enthralling. Like a demon or an angel or a demon possessing an angel. His movement speaks to me in a language I've never heard before but that I understand fluently. Serge is taking the audience on a strange, gut-wrenching journey to a sad, isolated place, a place called Solitude. His lines are perfect up there, but there's a wildness to his perfection that literally takes my breath away.

Tears are streaming down my face as the music ends, and I finally remember to exhale. I feel like a traitor, but I jump to my feet to join the standing ovation anyway. Out of the corner of my eye, I see that Mom Kelly looks practically murderous.

I can't stop staring at Serge, who moments ago was larger than life. He's normal-sized again now, panting and sweaty. He seems disoriented, surprised to find himself on stage in front of an audience. The theater's so small, I can see each bead of sweat on his perfectly toned, almost naked body, and I want to drink it, drop by drop, lick it off his skin. I feel parched just looking at him.

The rest of the showcase is a blur.

When it's over, the dancers come out of the backstage area through the wings and hop off the end of the low stage right into the audience. I see Renee rush over to Cam and hug him. They look serious for a minute, and then Cam makes his way over to us, stopping here and there to accept compliments from some of the other dancers' parents. While Mom Kelly and Mom Rachel take their turns congratulating him, I notice that Serge looks a little lost. He's put on pants but no shirt, and I wonder if that's why nobody's hugging him and telling him how great he was. They probably just don't want to have to touch his sweaty bare torso. I feel like I wouldn't mind it, though.

"So?" Cam says, looking at me. I realize I've missed my cue to tell him he was awesome. "What did you think of the show?"

"It was really good," I say. I lean in for a weird little embrace. "Both your dances were beautiful, as always."

Cam smiles and looks over at Serge. "How about Serge, huh?" he says a little wistfully. "Brought the house down."

"Oh, please," Mom Kelly says. "What *was* that? I came here to see ballet."

Mom Rachel shrugs. "I enjoyed it," she says.

"He was brilliant." Cam sighs. "Stole the show."

"His dance was really different," I say. "I think everyone was just surprised."

"I'm going to go congratulate him," Cam says. I guess he's noticed that nobody's approaching Serge too. "Be right back."

I watch Cam walk up to Serge and put a hand on his arm. Serge looks surprised and then shy and then happy. They hug briefly, then Cam's leading Serge over to where we're standing, his arm draped around Serge's bare shoulders. They're both laughing.

"Great job tonight," Mom Rachel says, reaching out to shake Serge's hand.

Serge looks a little flustered but thanks her politely.

"Yes," Mom Kelly says. "That was very…interesting."

Serge looks at me, but I'm mute. I just stare at his eyeliner, which he's applied with a heavy hand for the occasion.

"Listen," Cam says. "We're going to go get changed." He kisses his moms on their cheeks. Mom Kelly acts like she doesn't want to let go of him, but she does. "Sulie, can you wait for me?" Cam asks. "My moms drove. I don't have my car here."

"Sure," I say. Of course, I'll wait while he changes. Again. I'm practically a dance mom at this point. Mom Sulie. "I'll be here."

I half expect Cam to have Serge in tow when he reemerges in his street clothes, and I tell myself I'm not at all disappointed when he doesn't.

"So how do you want to celebrate another amazing performance?" I ask him. "Pizza again? Or Tony Baloney's?"

"Actually, Serge invited a few of us over to his place. Kind of a mini cast party. I was thinking we could go."

"Huh. You know what? I'll drop you off. Really. I don't mind. You should totally celebrate with them, and we can do Tony Baloney's some other time."

"Come on, Su-Su. Come with me."

"I don't want to."

"Why not?"

I sigh. "No offense? But I kind of hate hanging out with your dance friends, OK? I always feel really out of place. It's, like, a bunch of beautiful ballet people and clunky old me."

Cam laughs. "You're not clunky. Or old. And they all really like you. They *want* you to come to this party."

"No, they don't."

"Yes, they do. They even said so."

"Mia? Mia said so? Mia Nardone The Dying Swan was all like, 'Oh, Cam-Cam, I really, really hope you bring your weird, dowdy friend to this party. It'd make my whole night…'?"

Cam laughs as he climbs into my car. "Well, no," he says. "Mia didn't say that. But Serge did. I mean, he didn't call you weird and dowdy, but he said I should bring you. Said he *hoped you would come*."

"Really?" Huh. Serge. The boy I practically just watched become a man on stage.

"Yes. So. Sulie? We going?"

"Yeah, OK. On one condition."

"Name it."

"Tell me this isn't going to be one of those occasions where you guys dance around the whole time and talk about ballet while I just sit there wondering which of the sharp objects within reach would end my life the quickest."

"I promise," Cam says. "It won't be anything like that."

He's lying.

I start the car, but Cam grabs my arm before we pull out of the lot.

"Sulie?"

"Yeah?"

"Was Serge better than me tonight?"

"No."

Now I'm lying.

"The Queen City people didn't stick around after the show. Renee said they had to be somewhere, but I don't know…"

"If she said they had to be somewhere, then they had to be somewhere. Cam, don't do this to yourself. Your solo tonight was the best thing I've ever seen you do. I'm serious. I've watched you for a long time, and your performance tonight was on a whole other level. You looked like a pro up there. Even I could see it. And Mom Kelly was crying her eyes out! There's no way anybody left that theater with so much as one negative thought about you."

"Yeah," he says. He smiles a little. "Yeah. I mean, I really did feel good up there."

"You really *were* good up there."

"I was."

"Forget about Serge."

"I will if you will." Cam cocks his head and raises an eyebrow at me. "Will you?"

Chapter Sixteen

Serge lives on Lake Norman, a huge man-made lake built by the power company that also happens to provide our area's wealthiest families with pricey waterfront real estate. I groan as we pull down a long driveway and approach the oversized, boxy, contemporary structure that is Serge's house.

Cam mistakes my disgust for admiration. "Great place, right?" he says. "Wait until you see the inside!" He hops out of the car and starts up the long staircase to the front door, and I follow.

Serge answers the door and shows us into his foyer. He's wearing a black turtleneck sweater, but it doesn't look soft and cozy like Grandma's crochet. It looks stiff, scratchy. A veritable hair shirt. "Sulie," he says. "I'm glad you could make it."

I can't tell whether or not he's being sarcastic, so I don't say anything back. I look around a little nervously. Serge's parents must be out; the dancers seem to have the run of the place.

There's music coming from somewhere just above us, and Cam says, "Oh my God! I love this song! Come on, Su-Su!" and heads up another staircase into a raised living area. I sigh and follow him, aware of Serge at my heels.

The living room is a big, wide-open space. A wall of floor-to-ceiling windows looks out over the lake. A rectangular white couch and a black shelving unit are the only solid-looking pieces of furniture in the room. Everything else—a large ovular coffee table, stacking end tables, lamps, and a fully stocked bar—is made of glass. Platitudes about people in glass houses come to mind.

You'd think because Cam and his friends are so into ballet, they'd all eat health food and sip kale smoothies around the clock, but this is not the case. These kids can *drink*. I don't normally party, of course, and Cam says he doesn't like to drink either, but he must be lying or unusually susceptible to peer pressure, because he always joins in, and tonight's no exception. There's some kind of mixed drink in his hand less than a minute after we walk in the door. Mia and James and Natalie are here, too, and they're all holding these classy-looking, grown-up crystal tumblers full of various concoctions designed to make them act extremely childish and stupid.

"You want a drink?" Serge asks me. He has a tumbler too, but whatever he's drinking, he's drinking it straight. No bubbly mixers or fruit juices for him.

"I'm driving," I tell him.

Mia pushes Cam onto the couch, nearly spilling his cocktail on the white upholstery, and climbs into his lap.

When you've spent time as a twosome under your kitchen table stealing your grandma's Sunday cakes and scratched each other's hard-to-reach poison ivy that summer you went to the stupid day camp you both hated and been broccoli together in an elementary school play about nutrition the way Cam and I have done, you can't fall in love with each other. It's impossible.

I know this. But that doesn't mean I'm not well within my rights to absolutely hate the sight of my best—my only—friend hooking up with a skinny bitch like Mia Nardone.

Another song comes on, and Natalie squeals.

"Yes!" Cam lifts Mia off his lap and jumps up. He and James bump fists and start doing this crazy, agonizingly stupid-looking dance that's all jerky elbows and knees. Natalie joins them and, after only a momentary pout about being thrown over for a goofy dance, Mia does too. The whole thing looks rehearsed, probably because it is, because this is what these guys do when they get time off from dance class: they dance. They obviously all know these moves and have done them together millions of times. Whether it's a popular line dance I've somehow missed out on or a dorkfest of their own creation, I don't know, and I don't care.

I stare daggers at all of them, especially Mia, whose bony knees and elbows look like lethal weapons as she brandishes them about. I wonder how someone as thin as Mia, who I've only ever seen nibbling leafy greens, finds the energy to dance so much in one night. It seems like she ought to be on the verge of collapse. She drinks, though, and alcohol is full of calories, so, unfortunately, I guess she'll live.

"You sure you don't want a drink?" Serge is watching me stare at Mia. He's not dancing the knees-and-elbows dance.

"I'm sure," I say.

"What did you think of the show tonight?" Serge asks me.

I've been so wrapped up in hating Mia and her knees and elbows that the Senior Showcase feels like something that happened a really long time ago.

"It was great," I tell Serge, suddenly feeling kind of shy and having to work up the nerve to make eye contact with him. I try to focus on his eye liner. "You were right," I say. "You are amazing."

Serge smiles and then looks embarrassed for letting me make him a little bit happy. "Thanks," he says and finishes his drink.

"I've never…no dance has ever…" I glance over at Cam. I feel really guilty for what I'm trying to say, but I also feel like Serge needs to hear it. The knees-and-elbows song is over, and everyone's freestyling to something else now. Mia's got both her legs wrapped around Cam's waist, and he's kissing her neck as they sway to the music, so I go ahead and try to find the words I'm looking for about Serge's solo. "I've watched a lot of dancing, right?" I say to him. "But I never really got it. I've never, like, *felt* anything about it before. Your performance really spoke to me." Now I'm the one who feels embarrassed, but I can't seem to stop talking. "I can't believe you choreographed that routine yourself."

Serge shrugs. "I just wanted to do something different," he says. "Something that was all mine. I'm so tired of letting Renee and Joshua speak with my body. They have nothing at all to say."

Serge goes to take a sip of his drink, realizes the glass is empty, and frowns.

"What did you think it was about?" he asks me.

"What?"

"My solo. You said it spoke to you."

I nestle inside my scarves, pull my sweater tight around my body.

"Loneliness," I say. "I thought it was about how much it hurts to be alone."

Serge blinks into his empty tumbler. He doesn't tell me I'm right. He doesn't have to.

James and Natalie are scrolling through Serge's apparently extensive music collection. "Here we go!" James says, and Natalie yells, "Yes!"

"I need another drink," Serge says as new music fills his living room. I hate him more than a little for walking away and leaving me standing there by myself.

"*Dirty Dancing!*" Mia shouts. "I love this soundtrack!"

She and Cam are already dirty dancing, so I don't really see what the big deal is. Now James and Natalie are grinding against each other too. I should leave Cam stranded here without a ride home. I really should.

"You don't dance," Serge says. It's not a question. He's back, fresh drink in hand.

"I don't dance," I say.

"You want to go upstairs?" he asks me.

I'm petrified, rendered incapable of speech.

He tries to smile. "We can go hang out where it's quiet or we can stick around here and watch these guys try to recreate Baby's big lift at the end of the movie. Your choice."

"Upstairs," I say. "Definitely upstairs."

Serge heads for a big, modern staircase, and I follow.

Serge's room is huge, but there's almost nothing in it. It's completely decorated in black and white, and there are no snapshots or stacks of books or piles of laundry to add any kind of color to the spartan space. There are right angles everywhere. A large window looks out over the lake. I stand in front of it, admiring the view, and he joins me.

"Nice pants," he says to me.

"What?" I look down. "Oh." I'd completely forgotten that I'd been barfed on earlier and had to change. "They're Cam's dance pants," I say. "I found them in the trunk of my car. It's a long story."

"Actually, I'm pretty sure they're mine," Serge says with the biggest smile I've ever seen him crack. "I loaned a pair just like them to Camden months ago and never got them back. So, I'd love to hear that story."

I'm so embarrassed to be standing in Serge's room, inadvertently wearing his pants, that I don't know whether to laugh or cry, but I find myself choosing laughter and telling him the story—the rather longish story—about trying to help out at the mission and getting pick-pocketed and barfed on and wanting to help Sarah get back into teaching. He's the first person I've told about any of it, and it feels really good to talk about myself, to find I have something to say.

"How did you get interested in that kind of work?" he asks me, so I tell him about the blessing bags and how one of the purses brought me and Brandi together.

"Do you believe in fate?" I ask him.

"No," he says.

"Me either," I tell him. "Or I didn't. Now, I don't know."

There's an awkward lull. I think about the possibility that some things in our lives are predestined, that my grandmother's sunflower bag was meant to make its way back to me. Serge sips his drink.

"So you just lost your grandmother?" Serge says. I'd tried to gloss over that part of the blessing-bag story, but he's turning out to be a really good listener.

"Yeah," I say, hugging her crochet to my body.

"What happened?"

"Cancer," I say. "She had cancer."

"That sucks," Serge says.

I nod. "My grandma was…special. So special. Everyone who knew her thought so. She loved life, and it loved her back, you know? She loved being out in the world and doing things. She traveled and baked and laughed more than anyone I've ever met. So she opted not to go through a bunch of treatments that probably wouldn't save her in the end. She wanted to be up and about and spend time with us and with her friends, to be herself for as long as possible. The last few months were rough, though. She deteriorated so fast, was in and out of the hospital a lot. She suffered so much. It was horrible to watch and know there was nothing we could do. My mother's a total control freak, and she couldn't control this at all. It just…unraveled her." I wrap my arms around my midsection, lean against Serge's window, press my forehead against the cool glass, and stare out at the dark lake.

"What about you?" Serge takes just half a step closer to me.

"I'm trying really hard not to unravel," I say, my breath fogging the glass in front of me. "I found her…" I don't recognize my own voice at this point. "I'm the one who found her, you know, the day she passed, and I just…I can't…I can't stop thinking about it." All the yarn in the world couldn't hold me together at this point.

"You're crying." Serge doesn't sound concerned. He's merely stating a fact.

A terrifying crash and a bloodcurdling scream rip through the glass house, and Serge and I both jump. He curses, and we run for the stairs.

In the living room, Cam's sitting in a pile of broken glass, covered in blood. James is shirtless, his T-shirt wrapped around Cam's forearm. The girls are shrieking and holding on to each other.

I drop to my knees on the polished floor in the middle of the broken glass and reach for Cam's arm where James's white T-shirt is quickly turning crimson. "Cam! Oh my God! What happened?"

"Sulie! Holy shit!" is all he says. He looks really pale.

James shakes his head. "Mia said, 'Nobody puts Baby in a corner,' and hurled herself at him out of nowhere," he says. "Cam caught her but tripped over the coffee table and fell right on top of it. The whole thing just shattered."

Serge disappears and comes back with some towels. "Let me see," he says. He peels back James's T-shirt to reveal a huge gash that runs almost from Cam's wrist to his elbow. It starts gushing blood again immediately. Serge tries to stanch it with a fluffy towel. Natalie screams like a bad horror-movie actress, and Mia hunches over and vomits. Repeatedly.

"Can you drive?" Serge looks at me.

"Yeah," I say.

"Go get cleaned up," he tells me. I look down and realize my hands are red with Cam's blood. "Where are your keys?"

"My purse," I say, pointing with a bloody finger. "The sunflower bag."

Serge nods. "Let's get him in the car. James, can you get an Uber for the girls or something?"

"Yeah," James says. "I'll take care of them."

"Sulie!" Cam looks like he's going to cry.

"It's OK," I tell him. "You're OK." Serge, James, and I all help him to his feet. The guys stagger toward the front door while I run to the bathroom.

The red on my skin looks even redder in Serge's pristine white bathroom. I can't bring myself to stick my trembling hands under the faucet, to wash so much of Cam down the drain, to see so much of him swirl around the sink and then disappear forever. I think about the blood that once pumped through Cam's amazing, kind heart winding up in a sewer full of feces and rats, and I panic. I start to lick my fingers clean instead, cringing at the salty taste of Cam's lifeblood at first, then warming to it. I savor every delicious drop.

"Sulie!" James is banging on the door. "You've got to go!"

Reluctantly, I use the sink, comforting myself with the thought that I saved most of the blood, took it in, and made it a part of me. There aren't any towels left that I can see, so I dry my hands on my sweater and run.

Serge and Cam are in my back seat. I feel like a chauffeur or a getaway driver as I slide behind the wheel. Serge has Cam's arm wrapped in bath towels and is holding it up over his head. Cam looks really woozy.

"Don't let him pass out, OK?" I say, meeting Serge's eyes in the rearview mirror. "Keep him conscious."

Cam whines that his hand is going numb and his shoulder hurts.

"We've got to keep this elevated," Serge says. "You really did a number on yourself here, man. You've lost a lot of blood."

"I'm just so glad Mia's OK," Cam says with a huge sigh. "Right? I mean, can you even imagine if this were her? If I'd missed her entirely? I'd never forgive myself." Cam sighs again and looks out the window. "She's so beautiful, isn't she? Mia?

She's so…long. And flexible. God, Mia's flexible."

"You know what?" I say. "Maybe it's OK if he passes out until we get there."

Serge laughs, then stops himself abruptly, maybe because he decides laughter is wildly inappropriate given the gravity of Cam's situation or maybe because he just doesn't want me to know I've amused him.

At the hospital, we park near the door, and Serge and I help Cam get out of the car. He hasn't passed out, but he's pale and glassy-eyed. We both put our arms around him and help him through the sliding doors to the emergency room. Inside, the bright fluorescent lights really make the deep-red stains all over Cam's shirt pop. I can't stop looking at them, then at his arm wrapped in bloody towels, then at his stressed-out face. I try really hard not to think of other hospital visits, of other blood stains, of a grandmother that modern medicine couldn't save. Now I'm afraid that I might be the one to pass out.

They don't make us wait long, probably because they don't want Cam bleeding all over their waiting area, and we help him into one of the small ER cubicles. The nurses ask us over and over again what happened, and I'm starting to worry that they think Cam hurt himself on purpose, but when he starts mumbling details about *Dirty Dancing* and describing flexible Mia and singing "Time of My Life" and Serge corroborates that they're dancers together and I corroborate that Mia is a freaking idiot, they believe us that the whole thing was a (completely stupid and avoidable) accident.

Cam needs stitches, obviously. Lots of them. This realization sobers him up pretty fast.

"I'm going to have a scar," he moans.

Nobody tries to tell him he won't.

The doctor who's preparing to sew Cam up sidesteps me and bumps into a tray of medical instruments that rattles loudly. "It's a little crowded in here," he says, frowning in my direction.

"I'll go," I say, but Cam grabs my hand and squeezes hard.

"No! Please stay, Su-Su. Please?"

"I'll leave," Serge says. He looks at me and shrugs. "I'll wait for you out front."

I don't watch the doctor stick needles in Cam's arm or sew his skin together. Am I annoyed that he let Mia do this to him? Yes. Do I want him to suffer for it? Yes. But not this much. Definitely not this much. He squeezes my hand, and I squeeze him back and maintain eye contact with him, and I swear I can feel every needle along with him, as plainly as if they were all being shoved into my own arm.

"Try to relax," the doctor says, and I get the feeling he's talking to both of us. "These things usually look worse than they really are. You're lucky you didn't damage a major artery."

"Thank God it wasn't my leg," Cam says. "Can you even imagine?" He's looking up at me with wild eyes. "Oh my God. What if it had been my leg?"

"It wasn't," I say.

Cam is pointing and flexing his feet while the doctor works on his arm. I don't think he even realizes he's doing it.

"Where'd you and Serge disappear to?" Cam asks me.

"What?"

"While we were dancing," he says. "What were you two up to?" He raises his eyebrows at me.

"Nothing," I say.

More eyebrows and the ghost of one of his grins.

"We were just talking," I say.

"What about?"

"Nothing. I don't know." My conversation with Serge feels like forever ago. My eyes flick toward the doctor, who's still stitching away at Cam's arm. Before Cam decides to look too, I meet his eyes again and offer, "We were talking about my pants."

"Your pants?" He's full-on smiling now, trying not to laugh.

"Well, his pants." I hold up my leg, show him what I'm wearing because, of course, how could he possibly have noticed when Mia was around? "I thought they were yours. It's complicated."

"Sounds very complicated," he says. Then, "Ow!"

"Sorry," the doctor says. "We're almost done here."

Cam's phone beeps. He lets go of me and fumbles one-handed in his pocket. It beeps again and again. He looks at the screen.

"Shit," he says. "You told my moms?"

"I texted Mom Rachel when we got here," I say, and he gives me a sullen look. "I had to, Cam! All I said was that you fell and needed a couple stitches in your arm."

"More than a couple," the doctor says, stripping off his latex gloves. "Twenty-two. Twenty-two stitches." He shakes his head at us.

I feel like he should be shaking his head at skinny old Mia Nardone. Somebody should put Mia Nardone in a corner.

"Mom Kelly is freaking out!" Cam says. "They're almost here. Can you go head them off for me?"

"Of course," I say. I suddenly feel kind of overwhelmed by everything: the sight of Cam on Serge's floor, covered in his own blood, his pale, shocked face in the back seat of my car, the needles we both suffered in the ER. I lean over awkwardly and kiss him on the forehead. He looks stunned. "I'm really glad you're OK," I say.

He grabs my arm, and I think he's going to say something profound, but he looks down at my sleeve and says, "Oh no! I'm so sorry about your sweater, Sulie. I bled all over it." There's a definite patch of dried blood discoloring the yarn. I pull my arm away and put my hand over the spot.

"It's OK," I tell him. "It'll wash out." But I don't really care if it does, don't even want it to. I love the idea that I can wear Grandma and Cam at the same time now. "I'd better go handle your moms."

I go out into the waiting area. Serge sees me and stands up, but before I can interact with him in any way, Mom Kelly is flying through the sliding doors screaming, "Sulie! Sulie! Oh my God! Sulie!"

She rushes at me so hard that I brace for impact, afraid we're going to have another emergency on our hands. She hugs me tightly, then steps back and grabs me by the shoulders, looking me up and down and giving me a little shake. "What happened? Is he OK? Are you OK? How did this happen?" She pulls me back in for another death-grip hug.

"Kelly," I squeak but can't get another word out.

Serge steps forward and gently pries her off me. "Camden's all right," he says. "He cut his arm. He's getting some stitches."

"Serge." Mom Kelly turns her attention to the boy whose performance had her gnashing her teeth just a few hours ago. She clearly hasn't forgotten that. Her tone is almost cold. "This happened at your house? I want to know everything. Right now."

Serge stays calm and starts giving her a somewhat sanitized version of the Mia-knocking-Cam-into-a-coffee-table story as a tight-lipped Mom Rachel approaches and wraps her arms around me.

"He's OK," I tell her. "Really."

"Of course he is," she says and tries to smile.

"So you had nothing to do with it?" Mom Kelly is narrowing her eyes at Serge.

"He wasn't even in the room," I tell her. "The whole thing was Mia's fault." So what if Cam was drinking and acting like an idiot as well? Mom Kelly doesn't need to know every single detail.

Mom Kelly looks back and forth between me and Serge for a few seconds, then decides that neither of us is the person she really wants to see, and says, "I want to see Cam," in a voice that implies, "I *will* see Cam *now*."

Never one to miss a cue, Cam comes through the waiting-room door just then, his arm wrapped in gauze, cradled close to his body. Someone has seen fit to dispose of his blood-covered shirt and given him a green scrub top to wear, so at least Cam's moms are spared some of the gore the rest of us had to endure. He's clutching some paperwork and looks pretty steady on his feet, and I don't know whether it's an act or not, but he actually seems OK. Mom Kelly hugs him until he asks her to please stop, and Mom Rachel frowns at all the paperwork and goes to talk to the nurse at the desk.

When they're ready to leave, Mom Kelly thanks me for taking care of her baby, and I tell her it was Serge who did most of the first aid, but she doesn't seem to hear me. "Do you need a ride?" she asks me.

"No," I tell her. "I have my car."

"All right," she says, hugging me again. She's the biggest hugger I ever met in my life. "Text your mom, OK?" she says. "I let her know what was going on."

"Great," I say. "I mean, thanks."

"Sorry about your table," Cam says to Serge before letting Mom Kelly lead him out the door. "I'll figure out a way to pay for it, obviously."

"Forget it," Serge says. "It wasn't my table."

"Let's go," Mom Kelly says, and she puts her arm around Cam to help him out the door even though he doesn't really seem to need her to.

Serge and I watch them go, listen to the automatic door hiss shut behind them, and then we both exhale loudly, which makes us smile.

"I'll drive you home," I say.

"Thanks."

I check my back seat for blood, but it looks clean. Serge is out a couple of bathroom towels, I guess, but they saved my crappy upholstery. And possibly Cam's life. I text my mom while the car warms up. "Cam's OK. Kelly may have overreacted. Be home soon." She doesn't text me back.

I go to put the car in gear, but I can't. Like, I physically can't use my hands all of a sudden. They're shaking like a couple of leaves in a Category 5 hurricane. And I'm breathing funny, gasping.

"Are you all right?" Serge asks me.

"Yeah," I say. "I just need a minute."

It's actually about fifteen awful, uncomfortable minutes before I can get a grip on the steering wheel and breathe like a normal human being again. Serge doesn't try to comfort me, which is good because he definitely can't. Nothing anyone could do or say will ever erase the image of Cam bleeding half to death that's burned itself into my brain.

Neither of us says anything on the drive back to Serge's house. Which is weird because there's so much to talk about.

"Do you want to come in?" Serge asks when I pull into his long driveway. The house is dark, and it looms over us. I can't tell whether he wants me to say yes or no.

"I can help you clean up a little, if you want," I say. "Then I have to go."

Serge winces. "I forgot about the mess."

"It wasn't too bad," I lie. "Well. Except for Mia's puke."

Serge looks completely disgusted.

He lets us into the house, and we both hesitate before climbing the steps to his living room. I feel myself starting to tremble a little. I don't know if I can handle seeing Cam's spilled blood all over the floor again.

"Come on," Serge finally says with a sigh. "May as well get this over with."

At the top of the stairs, he flips a light switch, and we both sort of recoil, expecting to see a mess of glass and bodily fluids. But the place is sparkling clean. The broken glass is gone. The blood and vomit have been expertly mopped up. Even the crystal tumblers have been washed and dried and lined up on the bar. Except for the big empty spot where the coffee table used to be and the scent of cleaning products hanging in the air, it's like nothing ever happened.

"James," Serge says with a small smile and a shake of his head. "Good old James."

"You owe him," I say.

"Do I?" Serge frowns.

"Yeah," I say. "You do."

I do too. I'm so happy not to be cleaning up Mia's barf right now that I could kiss that beautiful, fastidious man.

"So what do you want to do?" Serge asks, and I realize I now have no good reason to be inside his house.

"I should go," I say.

"Do you have to?" he asks.

"Yeah," I say. "My mom will be worried." Lie.

Serge reaches for me, then stops. He shoves his hands into his pockets. "You and Camden," he says. "That's weird, right?"

"Weird?"

"Yeah."

"I guess," I say. "If being friends is weird." I meet his gaze almost defiantly; he isn't the first person to suggest Cam is too cool to hang around with me.

"You and Camden are friends," Serge says.

He's not asking, but I nod anyway.

"Just friends?"

"Yes." I swallow hard and feel my breathing quicken.

Serge's unblinking, expertly lined eyes are locked on mine. He leans in and reaches for my neck like he might want to kiss me, but he just gets a handful of scarf as I pull away from him a little.

"Don't," I say. "I mean, I'm not...I can't compete with all the ballet hardbodies you know." I'm embarrassed as soon as it's out of my mouth.

Serge closes the distance I've put between us. "Why do you and Camden think everything's a competition?" he asks gently, smiling just a little bit.

I don't know how to answer that. "I have to go," I tell him.

"All right."

He walks me to the door.

"I want my pants back," he says matter-of-factly.

"What?"

"You're wearing my favorite dance pants, and I want them back."

"Like, right now?" I am *not* stripping down to my underwear on Serge's porch.

Serge smiles like he's winning at some game, which, to be fair, he clearly is. "No," he says. "Not right now. Tomorrow's fine. I'll give you my number. You can bring them by."

I surrender my phone a little sulkily. "I have plans tomorrow. A campus tour and lunch."

"Then text me after lunch," he says. "I'll be waiting."

Chapter Seventeen

I feel nervous as I head over to the UNC campus. What if all the college kids can tell that I'm still just a lowly high schooler? What if I ask Brandi a lot of stupid questions about campus life? What if I clam up and can't find anything to talk to her about at all?

We've agreed to meet in front of the Student Union building because Brandi says I can't miss it, and she's right. It's huge. She waves at me from the steps as I arrive.

"You made it!" She sounds genuinely happy. "And you're wearing your own pants!"

I laugh and tell her the story about how the dance pants I thought were Cam's really turned out to be Serge's, and I unwittingly wore them to his house. She cracks up and claps her hands together, and all my worries about my conversational shortcomings vanish.

"Your friends are all dancers?" she asks as we walk.

"Well, just my one friend. The other dancers are his friends," I clarify. But I think about Serge listening to me talk about my grandmother, and I feel my heart flutter just a little as I wonder whether that's still entirely true.

Brandi is a great tour guide. She shows me where she takes a lot of her classes and walks me past the library. She lives at home because she was helping look after her mom, but she knows a lot of people who live in the residence halls. She has some friends buzz us in, and they let us take a look around. Some of the suites are really nice. I wonder what it would be like to live there with loud, messy roommates instead of at home with my neat-as-a-pin mother, walking past Grandma's redecorated-in-all-white room every night on my way to bed.

For lunch, we grab burgers. Brandi runs into a couple of friends who ask us to sit with them, so we do. Brandi introduces me as her new coworker, which makes me feel really grown up. Her friends are all really nice to me and treat me like one of the group. One of the girls compliments my shawl, and another asks where I got my cool shabby-chic purse. Some of them are going to see a movie later and ask us if we'd like to come. Brandi leaves it up to me, and I say that I can't because I have to go return some guy's pants. All the girls give me a knowing, sympathetic look before Brandi and I exchange glances and crack up, and I tell them the pants story.

It's a long walk back to my car, and I take my time, people-watching as I go. I can't believe how huge the place is, how many people are living and working and studying together here. I try to picture myself being a part of it next year. I'm not sure I can. I think that's why I waited so long to apply, to formulate any kind of a plan for life beyond high school, because I really have trouble picturing myself fitting in anywhere in the world, with anyone besides Cam.

I mean, if you've only ever had one friend, and he's definitely going to be dancing in a Charlotte-based company, then you just can't apply to schools out of state, right? So I never let myself really think about college too seriously until Brandi brought up UNC, which feels like a perfect compromise. And now, I realize, I fit in with Brandi. And I'm starting to fit in at Mission Possible. So maybe I could do this. Maybe, while Cam's tripping the light fantastic across town, I could be on campus, learning how to be a social worker. While he basks in the glory of audiences applauding his every move, I could be very happy too, learning how to make the small differences nobody ever notices. The kind that add up to big differences.

When I text Serge to tell him I'm done at UNC, he texts me back immediately. "Come over," he writes. "And don't forget my pants."

He meets me at the door, and I hold his pants out to him.

"Thanks," he says, half smiling. "Come in."

I hesitate. I already gave him the pants. I could leave right now. But I don't want to.

"Thanks," I say and step into the house.

Serge's living room looks different in the light of day without all the knees and elbows flying everywhere. It's much brighter, less cold- and indifferent-looking. And the daytime lake view is absolutely spectacular. There's still a conspicuous vacancy where a coffee table should be, but, otherwise, the room looks like it should be in a decorating magazine.

"What did your parents say about the busted table?" I ask Serge.

"Nothing," he tells me.

"Nothing?"

He shrugs.

I'm shocked. "My mom would have been super pissed."

Serge shrugs again. He seems unconcerned about other people being pissed, and I guess I'm not surprised. "Can I get you anything?" he asks me. It sounds so formal and adult. I feel weird.

"No, thanks," I say. "I just ate."

Serge plops down on the white sofa and tosses his black dance pants over the arm. I sit next to him but not too close. I can still see Cam on this sofa, Mia straddling his lap. I tug at my shawl a little.

"Do you make these?" Serge asks, reaching over to finger the edge of the shawl. "All these sweaters and scarves and things that you've been wearing?"

"No," I tell him. "My grandma did."

Serge nods. He doesn't say they're really nice or that my grandmother was clearly very talented the way a normal, polite person would. "I feel like I owe you an apology," he says instead.

"For what?"

"Last night. You told me some important stuff about your grandmother, and I just…froze. I didn't know what to say back to you. And then Mia almost killed Camden and there was the whole hospital thing and I just…let it go." Serge is staring right into my eyes in that disconcerting way of his. He's definitely wearing eye makeup, and he definitely didn't have a show today.

"It's OK," I say. I'll say anything right now to get him to look away from me, to stop staring into the depths of my soul in a way that's so mesmerizing I can't break our gaze.

"No, it isn't OK," he says. "I didn't even say that I was sorry for your loss. Which I am. I'm very sorry for your loss."

"Thanks."

"I lost somebody too," he says.

"You did?"

"My father. My dad. A couple years ago. But it was hard. It still is. I miss him every day." Serge seems nervous and choked up, and I can tell he doesn't talk about this stuff, like, ever, so I reach for his hand, and he lets me hold it.

"How did he die?" I ask.

"Car accident. On 77. They said it was instantaneous. He didn't suffer. They never explained the crash, though. He swerved for no apparent reason and was hit by two huge trucks, and nobody will ever know why. Did he fall asleep? Was he distracted? Did he do it on purpose? He just never came home."

"I'm very sorry for your loss."

"Thanks."

We sit in awkward silence for a while. A boat cruises by on the lake outside the window in my peripheral vision.

"What did you do with him?" I finally ask.

"Who?"

"Your dad. After he died, I mean. What did you do with his body?"

Serge looks at me like I've lost my mind. "We buried it," he says. "In a cemetery in Virginia where his parents are buried. And we put up a big marble headstone."

I nod. "That makes sense," I say.

"I'm almost afraid to ask," Serge says. "But what did you do with your grandmother?"

I let go of Serge's hand and reach into my sunflower bag. I pull out my rainbow-striped loot sack and show it to Serge. I'm careful not to spill ashes on his white couch. "I haven't done anything with her yet," I tell him. "At least, not with my portion of her."

I tell him about Grandma's last wishes and how her friends are all taking her fun places and how she's part of the flower boxes at Tony Baloney's and how Gordo knows just the place for her. I tell him that even Cam knew immediately what to do with her ashes, but I'm stumped.

"First," Serge says. "Remind me never to eat at Tony Baloney's." We both smile. "Second, your grandmother sounds like a very unique person. Just like you."

I blush and shove Grandma back into my purse. "She was unique," I say. "I just wish I knew what to do with her."

"You do," Serge says simply. "Look inside yourself. You know."

Inside myself. He might be on to something.

"I should go," I say and stand up.

Serge looks upset.

"Did I say the wrong thing?" he asks, standing up. "Are you mad?"

"No," I tell him. "I just…I just realized that I do know what to do with these ashes, and I need to go take care of it. Right now. Alone. Today. Today is Sunday. It has to be today."

"All right."

At the door, we share the world's most awkward goodbye, and Serge gives me a brief, firm hug. When he lets go, he frowns down at the bulky shawl and the tangle of scarves between us. "You're wearing all this to keep your grandmother close, and I get that," he says, trailing his finger down the length of one of the scarves. "But it's keeping other people away too."

When I get to my car, there are tears running down my face, and I don't really know why.

When I get home, my mom's MIA. That's good, I think, because then I don't have to explain what I'm doing. I go to the pantry and take Grandma's apron off the hook where it's hung for as long as I can remember. My mom must have overlooked it during The Purge. Or maybe there's just the tiniest possibility that she likes seeing it there as much as I do. I tie the apron on over my shawl and my scarves, and I'm so wrapped up in Grandma I could cry again.

I dig through the kitchen recipe box until I find the discolored, smudged index card labeled "Sunday Cakes!" in my grandmother's exuberant handwriting. I'm nervous and excited as I gather ingredients, measure, mix, and stir. I hum "The Dock of the Bay" to myself as I work, trying to recapture some of the magic of the other night. When the batter's ready and the oven's hot, I take my party bag full of Grandma out of my purse and, before I can think about it too much, I dump her into the mixing bowl and stir. My portion of the ashes is pretty fine, but their addition does make the batter look grey-flecked and strange. I add a little bit of oil to the recipe to make sure the mixture won't be too dry and stir some more. When she's pretty well blended in, I divvy the batter into Grandma's tiny cake pans and leave the oven light on as they bake so I can watch them rise. When they're done, I whip up some frosting and smear a sloppy lump atop each cake. I don't have time to wait for them to cool or decorate them carefully, so they look like a total mess. But that's OK. Grandma and I? We've always been OK with messes.

I sit down at the kitchen table with Grandma's apron still on and start eating. Fresh tears roll down my face with every bite, especially when I feel some sandy-textured gains between my teeth, which I figure must be Grandma Nell. I force myself to keep eating, though. Unlike all her other friends and loved ones, I cannot let Grandma go. I need her here with me, need to make her a part of me. I picture my body absorbing some of the minerals from these tiny bits of bone, picture the ashes being digested and turned into new cells inside my own body. I tell myself that, in this way, my grandmother still lives. In this way, I can hold on to her forever.

I sit there, sobbing and eating and sniffling and humming "The Dock of the Bay" until the cakes are all gone. I'm still sitting at the table with frosting on my face and hands when my mother comes in.

"Oh!" she says. "Sunday cakes!"

She takes a look at me and my nervous-breakdown face and all the empty cake pans around me and says, "Sulie? Did you just eat a whole batch of little cakes?"

"Yeah," I say. "Sorry. I'm going to make more, though. I'm making some more right now." I start measuring flour so she'll believe me.

"You don't have to make them on my account," my mother says a little stiffly, clearly hurt that I didn't save her any of the first batch. "But maybe you should bring some over to Camden."

"Cam?"

"Yes," she says. "I was just over at the McLarens'. His arm's still really bothering him." My mother looks at me closely. "That was a pretty bad cut, by the way," she says. "I didn't realize it was so serious. He just…fell over dancing?"

I nod and turn on the mixer so we can't talk anymore. My mother takes the hint and goes to her room. I know I should be nicer to her. I leave a plate full of my messy cakes as a peace offering. The messy kitchen I also leave for her to deal with is probably going to really upset her.

I take a plate of cakes over to Cam's. Mom Kelly answers the door.

"Sulie!" she says. She lowers her voice. "It's bad," she stage whispers. "He can hardly move his arm, and that audition is Thursday!"

"Mom!" Cam sounds exasperated as he comes up behind her. "I'm fine!" He waves his injured arm around. I can tell it hurts him, but only because I'm watching his face really carefully. "See?" he says. "Everything is fine."

"Here," I say, handing him the cakes.

"Are these Sunday cakes?" Cam looks floored.

"Yeah."

"You baked these for me?"

"Yes."

He sets the plate down and dives in for a one-armed hug. "You're the best," he says. When he looks at me again, his eyes are wet. "I thought you were mad at me, Su-Su. I've been freaking out all day, trying to figure out how to apologize."

"Mad at you?"

Cam picks up the plate of cakes and heads toward his room, and I trail along behind him.

"Yeah," he says, closing his door and plopping down on his bed. He pulls the plastic wrap off the plate in his lap and grabs a cake. "Last night, you, like, saved my life, and then I didn't hear from you at all today," he says around his first bite. "God, these are good."

"I'm sorry I didn't call you," I say. I honestly don't know why

I didn't. "I was busy. And I figured Mia might be here licking your wounds. And maybe some other parts of you too, even, given that she's the one who wounded you."

"You sound mad," Cam says, squinting at me and taking another huge bite of cake.

"Why would I be mad?"

"Because I acted like a total ass and basically ditched you at the party? And then I almost bled to death and interrupted whatever you had going on with Serge?"

I sit down next to him and pretend to think this over.

"You're right," I say. "Come to think of it, I'm furious at you for almost dying."

Cam smiles at me.

"Want a Sunday cake?" he asks me.

I've already eaten a whole batch plus part of a human being, which, if I'm being honest, isn't sitting particularly well in my stomach, but nobody can say no to one of Grandma's Sunday cakes. We chew quietly together.

"I really am sorry," he says.

"It's OK," I tell him.

"I haven't heard from Mia or Serge either," he says. "I'm going to have to apologize to them too, I guess. Only James has texted me today to ask how my arm is doing. Oh. And Natalie." He makes a face and reaches for his phone. "She sent me this."

I squint at the screen. I might be looking at an extremely blurry, poorly lit shot of Mia flying into Cam's arms moments before they smashed through the coffee table, but it's really hard to tell because nobody's head is even in the photo. "I mean, why would I want a picture of this?" Cam tosses the phone aside.

"Well, Natalie's obviously an idiot, so forget her. But Serge isn't mad," I say and then realize I shouldn't have. "And Mia's probably just embarrassed."

"How do you know Serge isn't mad?" he asks, grinning and looking at me sideways.

"I don't, I guess," I say. "All I meant was, he didn't seem mad last night."

"OK. And Mia?"

"She flung her drunk-ass self at her boyfriend and almost sliced him to pieces, then barfed all over the crime scene. Trust me, if you haven't called her yet, she's dying of embarrassment right now and is probably worried sick that you hate her. You're going to have to be the bigger person and reach out first to let her know that everything's OK."

"I'm not her boyfriend," Cam says.

"Yes, you are," I tell him.

We eat the rest of the cakes.

"Where'd you go today?" Cam asks me. "Your mom said you went out."

"I just had some stuff to take care of," I say. "Stupid stuff. Errands, mostly." I lie back on Cam's bed and close my eyes. I'm too tired to tell him about UNC and Brandi and Serge's pants. I'm suddenly exhausted. And warm. Hot, actually. Overheating. I take off one of my scarves. "I'm sorry if you were lonely today," I tell him. "We can do something after school tomorrow, if you want."

"I can't," he says. "I have to get some extra practice in before my Queen City audition. Joshua booked us a studio for the entire afternoon and evening."

"What about your arm?"

Cam shakes his head and sighs. He lies next to me so we're side by side, staring up at his ceiling. "They gave me some pain killers," he says a little sadly. "The show must go on."

"That it must," I agree, and we sigh heavily, both of us alone together.

Chapter Eighteen

Exams are over. Cam is celebrating because he never has to take another final as long as he lives. He needs to finish one project, and then he's done with high school forever, his transcript full of straight As. I'm trying not to think about the hit my own grades have taken. I've done the math, and I think my GPA will still be above the UNC Charlotte average, though. Between my test scores and my essays, I think I still have a pretty good shot at getting in…which makes the rest of senior year feel somewhat irrelevant.

We're pretty much all just killing time before winter break. Cam's arm is the talk of the school. Everyone wants to look at his stitches and hear him tell the story. I know it makes me a bad friend, but a very tiny part of me enjoys watching him blush and try to make the accident sound cooler than it was, mumbling something about a house party getting out of control. The phrases *Dirty Dancing* and "Time of My Life" never cross his lips once.

Jack Bramovitch thinks Cam's scar is going to look "bitchin," and, at lunch, a bunch of the guys start rolling up their pants legs and lifting their shirts right in the middle of the cafeteria to show off some of their own stupid-boy scars. They've fallen off rock faces and crashed dirt bikes and slid into home plate. They've run over each other with homemade go-karts and fallen off each other's roofs. After spending the entire period eavesdropping on the stories behind their injuries, I think it's a miracle that the human race has survived this long, that any males of the species ever live long enough to reproduce.

After school, I walk Cam to his car. "Are you sure you should dance today?" I ask him. I'm mostly being selfish. I really don't want to go home alone.

"I have to," he says.

"How's your arm?" I ask him. "Really?"

"It hurts," he says, flexing it a little. "I think it's mostly stiff. It'll work itself out. I was able to do some leg and core work last night, and it went OK."

"I miss you," I say as he tosses his books into the trunk where they land next to the gym bag full of dance stuff that makes its permanent home there. I know it's not fair, but I say it anyway.

"I miss you too," he says. He shuts the trunk and leans up against it, serious-faced. "How are you doing? I mean, about your grandma? Have you figured out what to do with her ashes yet?"

I shake my head. I'm not intentionally keeping the truth from him. I just don't have the words, not now, not here in the chilly school parking lot. And maybe I never will. Maybe sweet, happy Camden McLaren would be appalled if I told him, would never understand why I did what I did. He would probably say my grandmother is a part of me in spirit; I doubt he would understand me wanting to actually consume her.

"Oh, Su-Su," he says when he sees me frowning. "Come here." He wraps his arms around me, pulling me up against his chest, so my face rests against his cold jacket. It doesn't make me feel better. I don't hug him back.

I pull away from him. "You should get going," I say. "I don't want to make you late."

Cam hesitates.

"Really," I say. "Go! I have some stuff to do too, so now *you're* making *me* late."

Cam knows I'm lying, but he says goodbye and drives off anyway.

I go home and settle into my crochet nest with my sketchbook. I want to draw Serge, but I can't. I have an irrational fear that doing so will jinx whatever it is that's been happening between us, and the thought terrifies me. So I start on drawing number one million and one of Cam. My hand feels oddly detached from my body, as if maybe that marauding axe man got me after all, and I'm surprised and then frightened to see Cam on the floor in a mess of glass and blood that appears on the page. His face is twisted, and his shirt is covered in dark stains. My heart speeds up, someone's screaming in my brain, but I can't stop myself from drawing this horrible thing.

When I'm done, the drawing is smudged and messy, and it causes me physical pain to look at it, so I rip it out of my sketchbook and crumple it up. I can't toss it in the wastebasket, though, can't throw my best friend in the garbage, so I shove him into Grandma's sunflower bag. Tucking him in there, safe where Grandma's ashes had been, calms me, and I feel myself start to breathe evenly again. While I'm at it, I flip back through my sketchbook, pull out all the upsetting pictures of my grandmother at the end of her life, and shove those into the sunflower bag too. I don't want to keep seeing these things in my mind, let alone on paper.

My phone rings, and my hand is still shaking a little when I answer it.

"Hello?"

"Sulie? It's Serge."

"Hi."

"Hi."

There is no good way to communicate the degree to which I hate awkward silences.

"So what are you doing right now?" Serge finally asks.

"Drawing," I say.

"Cool," Serge says. "What are you working on?"

"Um…"

"Another picture of Camden?"

I can't tell whether he's kidding or not.

"Not really," I say, which is the lamest answer ever.

"Can you take a break?" he asks. "We could go for coffee…?"

I create my own awkward silence while I mentally weigh the relative ease of staying in my crochet nest against the certain discomfort of Serge's penetrating gaze.

"Sulie?"

"Do you know Café 105?" I ask him.

"Exit twenty-five?"

"Yeah. How about I meet you there in, like, fifteen minutes?"

"It'll take me a little longer than that, I think," he says, "but I'll be there."

Café 105 is always warm and good-smelling, and they have

these big, comfy booths to sit in. It's pretty much the perfect place to draw. I'm glad I get there before Serge so I can settle in with a giant latte and my sketchbook. I pick another customer at random, a guy with curly hair and glasses, and start drawing, trying to erase the picture of near-death Cam that's still burned into my mind's eye. If I just keep focusing on this guy's hair and glasses, maybe I can keep all the bad images my mind's been hoarding at bay for a while.

Serge scares the crap out of me when he sits down.

"Sorry," he says when I jump.

"You snuck up on me," I say.

"I said your name, like, three times." Serge looks amused.

"Oh," I say. "I guess I spaced out."

"Can I see?" Serge points to the sketchbook, and I hand it over. He looks at the picture, then looks over his shoulder at the guy in real life. "He's not attractive," he says. There's a question in his eyes, but not his voice. I'd probably answer it if I knew what the hell it was.

"No," I agree. "I guess he's not." I take the book back and shut it, stuff it into the sunflower bag.

Serge has already gotten his coffee and two big cookies. "Do you like chocolate chip?" he asks, passing me a cookie.

"Yeah. Thanks," I say. I feel weird taking anything from him.

"So how are you doing?" he asks.

"Good," I say. "You?"

"Good."

We try to cover up the silence by eating and drinking.

"How did it go with the ashes yesterday?" Serge asks me. "Can I ask what you did with them?"

"I ate them," I say and wait a second for that to sink in. "I baked them into a bunch of little cakes and then I ate them."

Serge looks at me for a long time, not blinking even once.

"That's messed up," he finally says and blinks twice.

"I know."

"Did it make you feel better?" He sounds like he already knows the answer.

"Not really." I hold his gaze, try to dilate my pupils, even, so he can see all the way inside my head. "It didn't make me less sad that she's gone, anyway," I amend. "But...I guess I'm glad I didn't throw her away or leave her outside somewhere cold or lonely. At least this way, I feel like she's a part of me."

Serge stares into my soul while I hold my breath just a little, then he nods slowly as if what I just said makes perfect sense. I wait for him to come to his senses, to get up and run screaming from Café 105, but he stays put. Sips his coffee, even. Nibbles his chocolate chip cookie. I just told him I'm practically a cannibal, that I eat dead people for dessert, and yet he's still sitting there, acting like we're a couple of normal kids out on a normal coffee date. It makes me laugh. And laugh and laugh.

"What's so funny?"

"Nothing," I tell him honestly. "Nothing in the whole entire world is funny."

When I stop laughing and dry my watering eyes on a napkin, Serge reaches across the table and takes my hand. There's a callous on my middle finger where I hold my pencil when I draw, and I feel him feeling it. I don't pull away.

"When my dad died, I got a tattoo," he says, turning his head so I can see the cross on his neck. Does he honestly think I hadn't noticed it before?

"OK," I say.

"He was religious, so I got a cross in his honor the day before the funeral. Right here." He taps his neck. "Where I can't help but see it whenever I look in a mirror. Which I do a lot, you know? I'm surrounded by mirrors every day at the ballet studio." Serge sighs. "But then, after the funeral, I realized I didn't believe in God anymore. I didn't believe in anything. I thought the symbol was completely meaningless. It didn't represent my dad; it didn't represent my deity. It was just a geometric shape. So I hated it, wished I hadn't gotten it. Then everyone at the ballet academy freaked out about it, said I ruined my look." He holds my hand a little tighter, and I find myself squeezing back. "When they started making me cover the tattoo up on stage, started making me pretend it didn't exist so I could blend in with everyone else and make other people feel more comfortable, that made me mad. And getting mad about covering it up made me realize that it did mean something to me. Maybe not what I originally intended it to mean, but still. Something significant." He looks almost hopeful, like he really wants me to understand. "Now, this cross is a reminder that I went through something tough, that I made bad decisions and went out of my mind with grief and ended up a stronger person for it."

"I like your tattoo," I tell him, and I mean it. I didn't like it five minutes ago, hated it a little bit even, but I like it now.

Serge smiles a little and looks down at our hands, still clasped together on the table. "It's OK to unravel a little," he says, "but you have to find a way to knit yourself back together."

My phone dings, and I ignore it. I don't want to let go of Serge's hand. It dings again. And again. But I can't let go of him.

"You can answer that," he says, and, to my chagrin, he lets go of me.

I dig my phone out of my purse and check my messages. It's Brandi. Sarah got the classroom assistant position, and they're going to go out to celebrate. They want to know whether I can make it. I tell them I can be there in an hour.

"It's Camden," Serge says.

"It's not Cam," I tell him. "He's at ballet."

"Really?" Serge frowns. "I thought he'd take a couple days off, let his arm heal."

"Days off?" I say. "Have you met Cam? He doesn't do days off."

"He said he saw you yesterday."

"You guys talked?"

"He called me to apologize." Serge shrugs. "I told him he had nothing to be sorry for. Then he wouldn't shut up about how you baked for him…" Something occurs to Serge, and he narrows his eyes at me.

"His were just regular cakes, I swear."

"OK."

I want him to reach for my hand again, but he doesn't.

"I'm sorry, but I kind of have to go," I say.

"Go where?"

I laugh. "Out for coffee, actually. Right now. This lady from the mission just got a job, and a few of us are meeting at a coffee shop in Uptown to congratulate her. That's who was texting me. It was Brandi, my boss. Do you want to come?" I don't tell him it will be fun or that he would really like Brandi because it might not be and he probably wouldn't.

"No," he says, gathering up our trash. "But I'll walk you to your car." If he minds me running out on him, he doesn't show it.

It's really cold outside, and I wish I'd worn more than just a sweater and one scarf. Serge takes my hand as we walk, though, and that makes me feel a little warmer. When we get to my car, he leans in and kisses me without warning.

It's a peck on the lips, really, nothing, just a momentary connection that he breaks before I even figure out how I feel about it. He pulls back and watches me. I try to have no reaction whatsoever. None. Even though I am absolutely dying for him to kiss me again.

"I want to see you tomorrow," he says.

"OK."

"I have ballet," he says. "Can I pick you up after that? We could grab dinner."

"I'll send you my address."

"OK," he says and turns to go.

"Serge, wait." I grab his shoulder. I just can't get in my car without taking some of him with me. He turns, surprised, and I kiss him, briefly but for real. He tastes like chocolate and coffee and something else that must just be him, and I lick the inside of his mouth hungrily, wanting to swallow as much of him as possible.

Chapter Nineteen

"**I** was the last interview of the day," Sarah says. She's beautiful right now, her cheeks flushed, eyes bright, interview suit still looking sharp. "They said they'd let me know, but I didn't think they'd call back just a couple hours later! I was shocked! I hardly even remember the conversation."

"Hey, girl, they knew a good thing when they saw it," Brandi says. "They'd have been crazy not to snap you up. Your resume is really strong, and you have a lot to offer those kids. You'll work your way up there in no time."

"I think it was this jacket," Sarah says, winking at me. "Sulie should be a celebrity stylist someday."

I blush. "Thanks," I tell her. "But I'm pretty sure it was your resume. I'm so, so happy for you!"

"Ahhhhh!" Sarah shouts happily. "I'm employed!"

We all raise our paper coffee cups in a toast that makes other people in the coffee shop look our way.

We say goodbye on the sidewalk, shoulders hunched against the wind. It's hard to watch Sarah walk away, knowing she's on her way to the women's shelter. She doesn't look homeless right now in her nice suit. I wonder how many other people out here on the bustling street look way better off than they are, and I shiver even more.

Brandi and I parked in the same garage, so we walk there together.

"Thanks for inviting me tonight," I say. "I only worked with Sarah that one time, but it was really great to get to help celebrate her success."

"One time, a million times, it doesn't matter. You helped her. She was right. Her suit looked good. You helped her, Sulie. Small differences." She smiles.

"I'm still kind of worried for her," I admit. "I mean, what if she's late commuting from the shelter or gets depressed again or just…you know…can't make it?"

Brandi shrugs. "We'll help her as much as we can," she says. "But she has to find the strength to pull herself the rest of the way up. Some people do, and some don't."

We walk the rest of the way to the garage in silence, the truth of her words weighing heavily on us both.

"This is me," I say when we get to my car.

"All right," Brandi says. "Well, listen, the mission's closed Christmas and New Year's, but if you're free in between, you're welcome to come help me close out a bunch of year-end stuff. Our clients typically don't have job interviews and stuff during the holidays, but we like to check in with everybody. You know, just tell them we're thinking of them."

"Sounds good," I say. "I should be able to help you out."

Brandi starts to walk away and then turns back. "Hey," she says. "How'd it go with that guy and his pants?"

I think for a minute. "Really good," I say. "I think it's still going."

"Nice," she says with a smile and a nod. Then, she's gone.

It's late when I get home. My mom's sitting on the couch with a cup of tea. "Want me to heat you up some dinner?" she asks me.

"I'm not hungry," I say, and it's true. I feel unusually full.

"Sulie?"

"Yeah?"

"What should I do with these ashes?"

I realize that some of my grandmother is sitting next to her on the couch. The little party bags that looked so festive in a big jumble in my purse look strangely forlorn individually.

"I don't know," I tell her.

"I feel like I have to hurry up and make a decision," she says.

"You don't," I say, and something in my voice surprises both of us.

I turn and head for my room.

"Where'd you go today?" my mom calls after me.

I turn around. "Nowhere," I say. Then I change my answer to: "Coffee shop."

I go to my room and see that there's mail on my pillow. Grandma Nell's friend May has sent me a letter with two pictures inside. One is of a whole bunch of Senior Stars, my grandmother included, sitting on a low rock wall in front of a sprawling view of mountains and a mist-enshrouded valley. The other is a picture of what I take to be May's back, waving her arms in front of the same panorama. An enclosed note explains that my grandmother loved the view at that highway overlook, that the Senior Stars always stopped to admire it whenever they took their tour bus west, and that she scattered my grandmother's ashes over the edge so that she can rest in scenic beauty and the Stars can visit her every time they pass through. I think that's absolutely lovely. I think I'd kind of like to visit her there too. I consider sharing the story with my mother, but it's been a long day and I'm really tired, so I tuck the note and the photos into my desk drawer and get ready for bed.

I lie in my pile of Grandma's handiwork, but I can't sleep. I want to sketch something, anything. I open to a blank page in my sketchbook and think about drawing Sarah radiant with the excitement of her new job, but it's Cam who appears on the page again. He's glassy-eyed and frightened, going into mild shock in the back seat of my car. Sweat stands out on his forehead; his face is almost wraithlike.

I'm practically hyperventilating, but I can't stop working until it's done. As soon as it is, I rip it out and ball it up and put it into my sunflower bag for safekeeping. I try again to draw Sarah, but it becomes another picture of Cam, lying on a hospital bed in the ER this time, gritting his teeth, his eyes screwed shut as the doctor works on his arm.

I can't take it anymore. The drawings are freaking me out. What Serge said about knitting myself back together echoes through my mind. I'm definitely starting to unravel. I climb out of my cozy nest and venture out to the hall closet, reaching all the way to the backs of the deep-set shelves in the dark, my groping fingers searching for the softness of a skein of yarn. I take it back to bed with me, but I stay awake and fool around with my old crochet hook instead of sleeping.

At school, I try to avoid Cam, but it's impossible because we have all of our classes together and sit right next to each other in every one of them. And because, you know, he's Cam.

"What's up with you today?" he asks.

I kissed your weird friend. Your ballet-academy rival. And I liked it. A lot.

"Nothing. I'm just tired."

And I want to do it again. Soon.

"You been up late sketching?" he asks. "Working on anything good?"

You. On the brink of death.

"Nah."

"I've just got one class tonight. Want me to come by after? We can go out for something to eat. Thai Kitchen? Or Souper Noodles? Come on! Souper Noodles would be sooooo good today." Cam clasps his hands and bats his eyes at me, pleading.

I'm going to eat with your rival. Your weird, intense, sexy beast of a rival. And you're not invited.

"Nah. I'm not really feeling up to it."

"Oh," he says. "OK." I know he's leaving a lot unsaid as well, and I feel really sorry to be disappointing him.

"Another time," I promise, but it sounds empty, even to me.

When I get home, my mom's in the kitchen, cooking. Something smells delicious.

"What are you making?" I ask her.

"Chicken soup," she says. "From scratch." She looks proud and kind of happy. "It'll be ready in time for dinner."

"Oh," I say, unable to hide my surprise. I can't remember the last time we had a real homecooked meal. "That sounds great. Perfect for this weather, even. But I can't...I'm going out for dinner."

"You are?"

"Yeah. I'm so sorry. If I had known you were cooking, I wouldn't have made any plans."

163

"That's OK," my mom says, but she turns off the burner under the soup pot. "What time is Cam picking you up?"

"What? Oh. Um. I'm not going out with Cam."

"Well, who are you going out with?"

"Someone else?"

"A boy?"

"Yes?"

"A boy who's not Cam?"

"Yes. I think…I think he's kind of my boyfriend."

My mom looks absolutely shocked. "I thought Cam was
your boyfriend," she says.

"No! That's…! Mom. We've never…! I mean…no! He's
not."

My mom looks devastated. I feel terrible. I hadn't realized
she hoped to be related to the McLarens someday. I have no
idea what to say.

"I'm sorry," she says, starting to cry. "I guess I just don't
know anything anymore."

She storms into her room, and I wait for her to come out so
I can say that I'm sorry again and tell her about Serge, but she
stays in there until it's time for me to leave.

When Serge's car pulls up, I run outside and jump into the
passenger seat so he doesn't have a chance to come to the door,
so my mother doesn't have a chance to hate him just for not
being her beloved Camden.

"Everything OK?" he asks me.

"My mom," is all I say. I shake my head. "Let's go."

"Where do you want to eat?"

"How do you feel about noodles?"

"I like noodles."

"There's this place called Souper Noodles just a few minutes away that is, like, beyond amazing."

"OK." Serge looks at me funny.

"What?"

"It's nothing," he says. "It's just…Camden asked me earlier if I felt like grabbing something to eat at this really good noodle place he knows called Souper Noodles. He and Mia and a bunch of other people were headed there right after class tonight. You guys are, like, psychically linked."

"No, we're not," I say. "And forget Souper Noodles then. Let's just find something in your neighborhood."

"Fine."

We end up with Chinese take-out that I know won't be as good as Souper Noodles.

"This smells good," I lie. I shift the bag on my lap as we go around a turn.

"We could have eaten there," Serge says.

"This is better," I say.

"You don't want anyone to see us together," he says.

"No!" I say. "Serge. That's not it. I just wanted to be alone with you."

We take another turn too fast, and the food bumps up against the door handle. When we get to Serge's house, he hits the brake too hard, and I feel my seatbelt strain.

"Serge?" I put my hand on his arm. "Listen, I've never had a boyfriend or anything before. Whatever this is, it's new. And I just need some time to get used to it."

Serge stares straight ahead. "I haven't had a girlfriend since my dad died," he says. "This feels new to me too."

He gets out of the car, and I follow him into the house. The place is dark and cold. I've purposely left all my scarves at home, and I regret it.

Serge turns on some lights, and I drop the bag of food on the counter next to a sloppy pile of mail. Right on top is a white bubble mailer from the dance academy.

"Hey," I say. "Is this the recording from your Senior Showcase performance?"

Serge glances at it. "Yeah," he says. "I guess it is."

"Can we watch it?"

Serge flips absent-mindedly through the rest of the mail.

"No," he says.

"No?" I'm disappointed. I want to see his otherworldly performance again. I want to see him shirtless without actually having to work up the courage to take off his shirt. I want to rewind and pause and see him move in slow-motion.

"No."

"Why not?"

Serge opens some of his mail. "Because," he says, sounding annoyed, "I can't, OK? I don't need to see all my flaws, all my fucking imperfections." He's getting really angry, intense.

"What are you talking about?" I ask. "You gave a flawless performance! Serge! You were perfection itself up there!"

Serge snorts. "There are no flawless performances, Sulie. There's no such thing as perfection. Not in ballet. Not in life. That's the best and worst thing about dancing, right? You're always striving for this unattainable level of perfection, and you know the whole time you'll never get there."

I just stare at him. I want him to know that I think he's perfect.

"Isn't it like that for you?" he says. "With your art? When

166

you draw Camden's face over and over and over again, isn't it because you're trying to get it just perfect?"

I think about that for a minute, and he lets me.

"I think it's more like I'm trying to capture all the imperfections," I say. "All the things that make it so unique and special."

Serge looks at me like I'm from another planet. I think he regrets bringing me here. I think he regrets knowing me altogether.

"Do you still want to eat?" I ask him. "Or I could just go…?"

He blinks and takes a deep breath. "Stay," he says. He starts shuffling through the pile of mail again. "Sorry. We can eat. Let's eat. I just…" He frowns at what looks like a power bill in his hand. "I have to pay this real quick. I keep meaning to do it and then forgetting."

He takes out his phone and starts typing. I watch him, watch the way he checks the invoice and then his screen and then clicks all the right links to transfer funds. It seems like a very grown-up thing to do, to pay a utility bill online.

"You pay the power bill?" I say.

"Yeah." He's done now. He sticks his phone back in his pocket and reaches for some plates.

"Your mom's not big on accounting…or…?"

"Yeah." He grabs some forks and knives from a drawer, rattling the silverware around more than is absolutely necessary.

"It's weird I haven't met her," I say. "Your mom?"

"Is it?"

"I mean, I've been over here a few times now, and I haven't run into her yet."

Serge opens the fridge and grabs two sodas.

"Does she work?" I ask him.

Serge sets down the sodas and looks at me. "No," he says.

"Serge?"

"She's in Europe."

"Oh," I say. "That's nice."

"Yeah."

"Vacation?"

"She's traveling with her boyfriend. He's a musician."

"A musician?"

Serge grabs the package with the showcase recording inside and tosses it to me. "He wrote the song I used for my solo," he says.

"Wow," I say. "He's talented." I set the package down.

"Yeah."

"So, will they be on tour for a while?"

"Yeah."

"When are they coming back?"

"I don't know."

"When did they leave?"

Serge stares at me, through me.

"Serge?"

"Six months ago," he says. His stare is icy, his body's rigid steel, but I see how unfathomably sad he is. I feel it, like I did during his solo in the Senior Showcase.

"She just left you?" I say, reaching for him.

Serge shrugs me off and starts setting the table. "I'm a legal adult, and she wanted to go," he says. "It doesn't matter, Sulie. Eventually, everyone leaves you."

I suck in my breath. I know he's saying that everyone has left him, or maybe making a general statement about how everyone leaves everyone else, but what I hear is, "*Sulie*, eventually, everyone leaves *you*."

"Serge," I say, but he ignores me. I feel myself starting to tremble a little, imagine Serge slipping away from me before he was ever really within reach. "Serge," I repeat, grabbing his arm as he reaches for the bag of food. "I'm not hungry."

He turns toward me, eyes fierce, his breathing a little heavy. "Well, I am," he says. "I'm starving." But he doesn't reach for the food this time. He reaches for me.

Serge kisses like he dances—no pretense, no fanfare. He's wild and perfectly imperfect. I swallow our commingled saliva, and it makes me want more of him. I'd like to eat his whole tongue.

We're shirtless soon, lying on Serge's nice white couch. My crocheted armor's been peeled away, and his painstakingly built muscles are tense. Serge shaves his body hair. I feel like this should be a turn-off, but it's not. He feels so much softer and smoother than I expected him to feel.

The lake ripples below us. I feel exposed. Serge swears no one can see us, says the lake's deserted this time of year anyway. He stops kissing me, panting, and holds my gaze. He reaches for the waistband of my jeans.

I can't breathe as he slides them down over my hips. I sit up, helping him take them off. Then, I reach for his waistband too. I take off his pants with trembling hands, and he watches me with those dark, penetrating eyes. His hungry gaze travels briefly up and down my body, and when his eyes return to my face, I feel seen for the first time in my life. There's something naked, raw in his expression, and I know I'm seeing all of him now too, and it makes me feel brave, confident, powerful. Serge. Surge.

We are people in a glass house, and nobody's throwing stones.

Chapter Twenty

When I get home, there's a note from Cam on my pillow. "Souper Noodles in the fridge for you. XO, Cam. PS: Boyfriend!?!?"

I feel like the luckiest person in the world because three different people have tried to feed me dinner tonight. And I haven't eaten any of it. And I realize I'm hungry. I'm starving.

I heat up the Souper Noodles, and they are super: long, slurp-worthy strands of pasta in a spicy, veggie-infused broth. I text Cam, "Thank you."

"Boyfriend!?!?" is all I get back.

I don't know what to write, so I write nothing. How could I possibly tell him about what just happened between me and Serge? Are there even words for the kind of connection we just shared? Could Cam of perfect, gorgeous Cam-and-Mia couplehood possibly understand?

But Cam's not going to let me get away with not answering, so he calls me.

"Boyfriend!?!?" he shouts as soon as I pick up. The funky punctuation is implied in his tone.

"You shouldn't talk about me with my mother," I say.

"Boyfriend!?!?"

"Cam. Relax. Up until a few hours ago, my mother thought *you* were my boyfriend."

"She did? Really?"

"Yes!"

"That's crazy."

"It is. She is. So don't pay any attention to her. OK?"

"OK."

We're both quiet for a minute.

"Is it Serge?"

"Cam!"

"All right!"

"I just wanted to say thanks for the noodles."

"You're welcome."

"How was class?"

"Good. I think my arm's loosening up a bit. It feels better."

"Tell me you have tomorrow off to rest up for your audition."

"No," he says. "But it'll be a light day. Renee just wants me to do some stretching and some barre work. She wants to give me some pointers, you know, because she danced with Queen City for so long. I need to do everything I can to be prepared."

"You'll do great," I tell him. I think about what Serge said, how no dancer's ever really good enough, and I wonder whether Cam thinks that too, but I don't want to mess with his head right now by asking him.

Wednesday's the last day of school before winter break and also the day before Cam's big audition. Everyone at school is wishing him luck, telling him to break a leg, telling him not to trip over any glass coffee tables on his way to the studio, har

har har. They all think it's awesome that they know a professional dancer. Nobody even thinks about dunking Cam's head in a toilet.

"Don't let Renee work you too hard," I tell him before he gets in his car.

All around us, kids are running for their vehicles, laughing, throwing things at each other, excited about the break. They act like they don't have a care in the world, but Cam is tight-lipped and nervous. He's not getting a break. Not yet. Not until he's absolutely sure he's gotten his Big Break, at least.

"Can I call you later?" he asks. "When I'm freaking out about tomorrow?"

"Of course," I tell him. "Just help me out here. If and when that happens, what would be the right thing for me to say?"

Cam half smiles. "Tell me I'm amazing and talented and special, all right? Just say it exactly like that. OK?"

"OK."

When the inevitable phone call comes, I'm at Serge's. We're curled up on the couch watching a movie. And maybe not watching it too. Maybe doing other things. Serge presses pause—on the movie and everything else—while I answer the phone.

"Sulie? I'm freaking out."

"You're amazing and talented and special, all right?"

Cam laughs. "Thanks," he says. "How did you know that's exactly what I needed to hear?"

"Cam?"

"Yeah?"

"They're going to love you."

"Thanks."

"Break a leg. And call me as soon as you get out tomorrow."

I look at Serge as I hang up. He restarts the movie but not anything else. We both pretend to watch it for a while. A comically dysfunctional family engages in holiday hijinks and other kinds of hilarity that ultimately, unbelievably, teach everyone the true meaning of Christmas.

"What are you doing for Christmas?" Serge asks me. He looks at the TV screen instead of at my face.

"Christmas?"

"Yeah."

"I dunno yet."

"Really?" He looks right at me now. "Christmas Eve is, like, two days away."

"It is?"

"Yeah."

"Oh." How did I not know this? "I hadn't realized. I, um. I guess we'll stay home. It was always just me, my mom, and my grandma, so I guess it'll just be me and my mom." I look around Serge's big, empty house, and something dawns on me. "You should come," I tell him, and he raises an eyebrow at me a little skeptically. "Yeah," I say, trying to reassure both of us that this won't be weird at all. "You should totally come."

When I get home, I ask my mom whether she knows it's almost Christmas.

"Yes," she says. "Of course, I know."

"Well, shouldn't we get a tree or something?" I ask.

"Do you want to?"

"Yes?"

My mother nods slowly.

"I kind of invited my boyfriend over," I tell her.

174

Her eyes get big. "Then we'll need a tree," she says. "I'll get my coat."

The closest tree lot is just a tent set up next to a gas station. It smells like diesel and pine sap. "How much for a seven-footer?" my mom asks the attendant.

"Fitty," he tells her.

That's not a number, but my mom nods at him like it is.

"How about this one?" she asks me.

"Fine," I say. It's late, and it's cold. "This one's perfect."

My mom pays the attendant, and he ties the big tree onto our car. Unfortunately, there's no attendant in our driveway to help us get the monstrosity into the house. My mom and I struggle and swear and wrestle the thing into a stand in the living room. By the time we're done, we're laughing and teasing each other. It's almost as if our holiday hijinks are teaching us the true meaning of Christmas. Life imitating art, I guess.

"We can decorate it tomorrow," my mom says once the tree is properly positioned and the stand is filled with water.

"Let's stay up and do it now," I say. I know that if we wait, we won't do it together. All the momentum we have right now will be lost. She'll wake up early and go out to run errands, and I'll work on it alone, or I'll go over to Serge's and leave her stuck with it.

"OK," my mom says. "There's no time like the present, I guess." She looks at the clock and shrugs. "Why don't you make us some cocoa? I'll get the decorations out of the attic."

Tree-trimming isn't the same as it used to be when Grandma Nell was alive because nobody's singing Christmas carols or passing around Sunday cakes to nibble on while we work, but it's not that bad either. My mom and I both admit we'd been avoiding thinking about the holiday because it's going to be really hard to get through it without Grandma Nell, and knowing that we have this in common makes me feel strangely close to her.

We hang all the same lights, the same old ornaments, and the same silver beads we've always put on our tree, but it does look different this year, less sparkly and less special. I run to my room and grab one of Grandma's shawls, wrap it around the base as a tree skirt, and the whole thing shines a little brighter. My mother nods quietly in approval.

"Have you done your shopping?" she asks me as we sip cocoa and admire our work.

"No," I say. "Have you?"

"Not yet."

My mother stares into the tree. "What about this boyfriend of yours?" she asks me.

"What about him?"

"Well, if he's coming for Christmas, I want to get him something. What's he like?"

I shrug. "He's into ballet." Sadly, this is the only thing I know about Serge that I feel like I can share with my mother.

Her face lights up. "It *is* Camden!" she says. "I knew it! Oh, Sulie, you really had me going for a while there."

I smack my forehead with my palm. Just when I think we're getting somewhere…

"Mom!" I tell her. "It's not Cam!"

"You know another boy who does ballet?"

What are the odds, right?

"His name is Serge," I tell her, and it feels so strange to hear his name out loud in my living room. "He's in Cam's ballet class. And." I give my mother a meaningful look. "You don't need to get him anything."

"Yes, I do," she says matter-of-factly. "And so do you, young lady."

And if I'd had any hope at all of being tired enough after our late-night, impromptu tree-trimming party to actually get a good night of sleep, my mother has killed it with that one, single, stress-inducing statement.

Chapter Twenty-One

I'm surprised to see the Christmas tree in our living room when I get up. Decorating it had felt almost like a dream. My mom's drinking her coffee on the couch, staring into its branches.

"Good morning," she says as I plop down next to her.

"Hmmm," I say. I'm not really a morning person.

I check my phone. No messages. It's nine o'clock. Cam's audition is supposed to start at ten. He must be arriving at the Queen City studios now, checking in, warming up. I have nervous butterflies in my stomach. I tell myself, "He's amazing and talented and special, all right?" but it doesn't really help much.

Serge texts me, asking if I want to hang out. I figure I may as well. I have no idea how long a dance company audition is supposed to take. I figure when Cam gets out, maybe we can all celebrate together. Even Mia and James and Natalie. I'm sure that all his friends will be as happy for him as I am. I tell Serge I'll come over. I decide I don't need to mention the rest of it yet.

The weather is gorgeous. Cold and crisp, sunny without a cloud in the sky. I feel strange. I feel almost happy.

Serge comes out to meet me in his driveway. "Aren't you freezing?" he asks me. I'm wearing just a T-shirt and jeans. All my shawls are at home.

"You can warm me up," I say, and he laughs and kisses me, before we hurry into the house.

"Do you want anything?" he asks me as we pass the kitchen, and I shake my head.

"Just you," I tell him, and we stumble toward his couch.

He's been kissing me and touching me for days now, but everything feels different today, better. I'm more in the moment, more aware of every little thing about him. The pressure of his fingertips, the smoothness of his back. His eyes are lighter too, less terrifying than usual. He's gone a little easier on the eye liner.

I've been pretty passive up until now, but today I take charge. I push Serge back onto the couch and climb on top of him. I kiss his face, his tattooed neck, his rock-hard chest. I kneel on his polished floor and reach for his pants.

"Sulie?" he says. I think it's the first time I've heard a real question in his voice, the first time he's really wanted to know something.

"I want to," I say, and he doesn't ask me anything else, just helps me take his jeans off. His hands grip my forearms as I go down on him, and I appreciate the connection as well as the nonthreatening nature of it. It suddenly occurs to me that I ought to be nervous, that I don't have any idea what I'm doing, that Serge could misinterpret my enthusiasm and get rough. I decide that if he grabs my head, I'll bite him, but he doesn't. He's gentle. I don't have anything to worry about.

It's uncomfortable to have him in my mouth like that, but I feel him tensing up, and the thought of what's going to happen is exciting enough to keep the experience from being entirely unpleasant.

Serge is a tough guy, but he's still a guy, and it doesn't take long to get him off. He doesn't moan or spaz out or do anything that I've seen men in similar situations do on TV. His orgasm is perfectly controlled, choreographed, almost, and suddenly I'm overwhelmed by the salty taste of him, and it's so delicious, so satisfying, that I want to cry. I'm surprised by the volume of it all, by how much of Serge there is to swallow. I drink him in greedily, take all of him I can get. I think I will never be hungry again.

Serge pulls me up onto his lap and holds me tight. "Sulie," he says, burying his face in my neck. I think he's crying. He doesn't say anything else.

We fall asleep wrapped around one another. When we wake up, some clouds have skittered across the perfect sky. Serge puts on his jeans and switches on a glass table lamp. He offers to make me a smoothie.

I feel disoriented as I pull my shirt on and follow him to the kitchen. "What time is it?" I say.

"One," Serge says. "Would you rather have lunch?"

"What? No," I say. "I have to check my phone."

No messages.

Serge pulls some stuff out of the fridge.

"How long does a ballet audition take?" I ask him.

He shrugs and starts the blender.

I text Cam. "Hey," I write. "You'd better not be celebrating without me!"

"Taste this," Serge says.

"Wow," I say. "That's…tart."

Serge laughs. "Give it back," he says. He adds some more juice and blends it again. "Better?" I give it another taste.

"Mmmmm," I say because I don't want to out and out lie. Thank God I'm not at all hungry, that I'm still full of Serge. He makes the worst smoothies ever.

"Cam?" I type. I pretend to drink my smoothie and wait for him to write back. "What's up?" I text. "Did you already forget all of us little people?"

"Come over." That's all he writes back. Which can't be good.

"Are you OK?" I type.

"Sulie?" Serge is looking at me.

"Huh?"

"Are you listening to me?"

"What?" I say. "No. Sorry. Hang on."

"Come over," Cam writes again.

Shit.

"Serge," I say. "I think I have to go."

For a split second, I can see how much this hurts him, how this cuts him in a way that no ER doctor could ever stitch up, and then his face is a steel mask again. He sets down his blender and says, "I'll walk you to your car."

He's still shirtless and barefoot and it's cold out and he's shivering and I just want to warm him up forever and ever. I think about trying to explain that I think Cam's audition didn't go well, but I don't even really know what's going on, and I don't know whether Cam would want me to tell people if I did.

I kiss Serge and run my hands through his crazy white-blonde hair before I jump in my car. "I'm sorry," I tell him. "I'm so sorry. I'll make this up to you tomorrow, I swear."

He doesn't say it's OK. He stands there in the cold and watches me drive away.

I'm forty minutes from Cam's house, but I make it there in half an hour flat. Mom Rachel lets me in and tells me Cam's in his room, and the way she says it…my heart sinks.

"Cam?" I tap on his unlatched door, and it swings open.

Cam's lying on his bed, his arm over his face. "I didn't get in."

"What?" I heard him, but what he's saying is completely incomprehensible to me.

"The audition." His voice catches. "I got cut after barre."

The audition was supposed to have three components: barre, floor work, and then a solo performance of the dancer's choosing followed by a personal interview. Cam was going to dance Albrecht again for his solo. He would have aced a personal interview.

"Oh my God, Cam," is all I can say. "That's crazy. They're crazy." I want to say the right things, but I don't know what they are, and I hate myself for it. "Was it your arm?" I try. "I mean, I'm sure it affected your dancing. Maybe you can get a doctor's note? Ask for a do-over?"

"It wasn't my arm," Cam says flatly. "My arm felt fine. It was me. They just didn't like me. I'm out. There are no do-overs."

Cam starts to flat-out cry, and I let him. This is some sad, fucked-up, cry-worthy shit for sure. I know he needs to be comforted in some way, so I lie next to him and reach for his hand. He holds on tight and sobs.

"I really wanted this," he says when he's calmed down enough to sit up and sniffle into a tissue I've dug out of the bottom of Grandma's sunflower bag.

"I know, Cam. I'm so, so sorry."

We're quiet for a while. I wish Serge were here because I'm positive he'd know what to do and say, how to take control of the situation and put this all into perspective.

"What does Renee say about this?" I ask him. Shouldn't his mentor be here smoothing this over, the lady who told him all year long that this audition was a sure thing?

"I haven't told her yet," Cam says morosely. "How can I? She wanted this for me so badly. It's her old company! She thought I was a shoo-in. She's going to be so disappointed." Cam pounds his fist on the mattress. "Fuck!" he yells. "I told everyone I was doing this! Everyone's going to be so fucking disappointed in me."

"No, they're not."

"They are! Mom Kelly is practically suicidal! She was crying and shaking..." Now Cam is crying and shaking. "This was my only plan!" he shouts. "I don't have a Plan B! What the fuck am I going to do next year, Sulie? Just sit around and do nothing like you?"

His words are a punch to my gut. They take my breath away, so it's a minute before I can respond.

"I'm not going to do nothing," I say quietly.

"I'm scared shitless," he says.

"Me too," I whisper. "And then some."

Chapter Twenty-Two

Cam eventually calls his dance teacher, Joshua, who's apparently really supportive and tells Cam that there are going to be a ton of open auditions in February and March, especially in New York, and that he shouldn't give up on his dream.

"New York?" I wail. I'm the most selfish person in the entire world because I suddenly don't care about his dream half as much as I care about him staying here with me. "You're going to go dance in New York?"

"If I'm lucky!" Cam says. "Or California! Or Oregon! Or Canada! I'll dance with anyone who'll have me! These open auditions are insane, Sulie. Cattle calls. So many people, the best of the best. At this point, I'll be vying for a place in somebody's B company, hoping I get a couple years to prove myself and move up. It's going to be so hard."

"You're amazing and talented and special, all right?" I tell him.

When I leave the McLarens', Mom Kelly is on the internet looking up open auditions and making a list of them by date and location so Cam can hit as many as possible. She's doing a really good job now of putting on her brave face for her son, and I surprise the heck out of her by sneaking up behind her and giving her a little hug of encouragement before I go.

Serge doesn't answer any of my calls.

So I go to his house.

He doesn't answer his door.

But Serge lives in a glass house, so I go out back and throw stones.

"You're going to break a window." He's stepped out onto the deck and is frowning down at me over the railing.

"Then let me in," I say. "Please?"

He nods, and I go back around to the front door.

We face each other in the foyer. Serge is wearing fleece lounge pants and a hooded sweatshirt with the hood up. His eyes are red and bloodshot.

"You spent the rest of the day with Camden," he says. His tone is flat; it's not an accusation. It's not a question either, but I feel like I have to answer it.

"Yes," I say. "It was an emergency. I'm so sorry."

I don't really want to tell Sege about Cam getting cut after barre because it's not my news to tell, but he's already guessed.

"He had his audition today," Serge says. "It didn't go well."

"No," I say. "It didn't. He's devastated."

Serge shrugs.

"You don't seem that surprised."

"I guess I'm not, but I'm really sorry it didn't work out for him."

"Well," I say. "You could knock the rest of us over with a feather. Cam, his moms, Joshua…"

"Camden…"

"Yeah?"

"Well, it's none of my business, but I never saw why he would want to dance with Queen City anyway."

"What?"

"They're so contemporary. Camden's so…classical. So Camden." Serge almost smiles.

"But Renee said—"

"Fuck Renee. Camden's her pet, and he does whatever she says. She wanted him to dance where she danced. It would have made her look good and kept her connected to her old company, but it wasn't the right thing for him. It wasn't a good fit. Camden's too careful in his work to fit in at Queen City."

I've never heard anyone criticize Cam's dancing before. On the one hand, I want to stand up for my oldest and dearest friend. On the other, I think that Serge might be at least a little bit right.

"Is this why you were trying to smash my windows?" Serge asks. "So we could talk about Camden's career?"

"No."

"Why are you here, then?"

I try to put my arms around him, but he pulls away from me, jams his hands into his sweatshirt pocket. "Sulie, don't," he says.

"OK." I take a deep breath. "I just wanted to say that I really care about you a lot and that even when I'm not, like, right here with you, I'm here for you. I felt like you might really need to hear that."

Serge just stares at me. He doesn't have any eye makeup on at all. He looks a lot younger like this.

"And I'm sorry I ran out on you earlier. I didn't want to go."

"We'd just shared…everything," he says. "It was…! I felt so…! I mean…I thought we were completely on the same wavelength. And then you just took off to go be with some other guy! As soon as Camden beckons, you go running."

"I've never had a lot of friends," I tell him. "Maybe I'm not good at managing multiple relationships. I've been really freaked out ever since Cam's accident, and I may have overreacted. I feel like I have to hold on to him really tightly, or he'll just…slip away from me." I'm crying now, and I don't even have any crocheted scarves to hide in. "Ever since my Grandma died, I'm so afraid someone else is going to leave me. And they are, right? Everyone is. Now Cam's going to go to New York. I mean, New York! And what about you?"

"Me?"

"I bet you're leaving next year too."

Serge looks at the floor.

"Where are you going?" I ask him. "Huh? New York? London? Ant-frigging-arctica?"

"Utah."

"Utah?"

"For college. Dance major. I got in early decision, full scholarship. I'm going to minor in business."

"Business?"

"I'd like to have my own dance company someday."

"You're leaving."

"I'm leaving here. But I'll be arriving in Utah." He looks at me with what might be an apology in his eyes, but he looks away before I can be sure.

"Well, I just want you to know that even if you're in Utah and something really bad happens like, I don't know, you get an F on

your plié midterm or you have a panic attack on the quad because you can't get your finance homework done in between
dance rehearsals, I'll be there for you. Like I was there for Cam
today. Like you've both been there for me lately. Like I would be
there for any friend whose whole world was falling apart."

"Because even when you're not, like, right here with me,
you're here for me."

"Yeah."

"As a friend."

"As whatever you want me to be."

Serge searches my face while thinks this over.

"Let's just be friends for now," he says, staring down at the
floor again. "I'm not as ready as I thought I was for anything else."

I leave Serge's house with most of my dignity intact, but I
have to pull over before I get on the highway because tears are
blurring my vision. It starts to rain while I'm parked there on
the shoulder, and it suddenly feels like the whole world is crying, like there's no happiness anywhere for anyone.

I finally make it home and try to distract myself with my
sketchbook, but it's Serge's face that keeps showing up now,
that wounded look he had in the kitchen when I chose someone else over him, the hurt on his face when I tried to
apologize, the raw emotion when he said we should just be
friends. It hurts me to draw them, but I can't stop myself, and
I rip each one out and crumple it up and put it in the bag with
all my terrifying Cam and sad Grandma pictures. I finally give
up and put my sketchbook away and reach for my yarn instead.

In the morning, I go to the McLarens' house, and Cam's
moms are both still in their pajamas when they do their cute
little answering-the-door-together thing.

"He's still in his room," Mom Rachel tells me. "He hasn't even eaten anything."

"Enough is enough already," Mom Kelly says. "Go give him a swift kick in the ass."

I've never heard Mom Kelly curse before. It's kind of exciting.

"I've got this," I tell them.

I bang on Cam's door.

He says, "Go away," but I open it anyway and plop down on his bed where he's still curled up under the covers.

"Here," I say, throwing a huge package at him. "I brought you a Christmas present."

"Is it a spot in the Queen City Company?"

"No."

"Then take it back."

"I can't. You have to open it."

Cam sits up and shoots me a petulant look. "Can't I just lie here and feel miserable?" he asks. "Everyone wanted me to take a day off. Now, I'm taking one, and my moms won't stop pounding on the door, and you just pop on in."

"You hate days off," I remind him.

His hair is matted, and there are bags under his eyes. He sighs miserably. God, his breath is even bad. I've never seen him like this.

"Here." I shove my gift at him again. "You're hurting my feelings by not opening it."

"It's not even Christmas yet." Cam flops back onto his pillow.

"It's Christmas Eve," I say. "Close enough."

Cam sighs and half-heartedly opens my sloppy wrapping, ripping it apart and tossing it aside, not even lifting his head from the pillow. I used almost a whole roll of paper, and I can see that this annoys the crap out of him.

"Oh my God!" He sits up when he finally sees what's under all the gift wrap. "Sulie! It's Grandma Nell's valise!" He runs a hand over the soft, perfectly worn-in leather.

This was the bag my grandmother took on all her adventures. She called it a valise instead of an overnight bag because she thought it sounded fancier, and Cam and I used to help her pack and unpack it and hear all about her trips. Well, maybe not *all* about them, since we never heard that Nashville story or knew that she'd taken belly dancing lessons until her funeral...

"You can't give me this," Cam says.

"I just did," I tell him. "I want to. My mom wants you to have it too. We never go anywhere but, Cam McLaren, you are going places."

"No, I'm not."

"You're going to New York," I remind him, trying to sound like I think that's a good thing even though I still wish he didn't have to go. "You're going to need something to carry all your tights and snazzy outfits around the city in. Tell me you wouldn't look awesome walking down the streets of New York with this vintage bag over your shoulder."

Cam is smiling just a little. "It *is* pretty perfect," he says. "What's this?" He caresses something soft and brown tied to the handle. I untie it and wrap it around his neck.

"It's a scarf," I tell him. "It's freezing up there. Way colder than here."

"One of Grandma Nell's?" he asks.

"No," I tell him. "One of mine. I've been trying to remember how to crochet. That's why it's kind of uneven and lumpy and weird in places."

"You made this for me?"

"Yeah. And by the time you get settled in up there next year, I'll be a lot better. I'll be able to send you, like, a million sweaters and hats. Maybe even some leg warmers you can wear to class."

"Great," he says. I can tell he hopes I'm kidding about all the crochet (I'm not), but he's smiling a real smile at me. "Thank you," he says. "It was really nice of you to try to cheer me up."

"It really was," I say. "So now you owe me a favor."

"What?"

"Yeah. See, I kind of forgot that it was Christmas? And now you have to help me do all my shopping."

Cam's moms love my ploy to get Cam out of the house, but he's not as impressed. "You're the worst cheerer-upper ever, Sulie. You know that?" he says. "There's absolutely no place less cheerful than the crowded mall on Christmas Eve!"

"It's not that crowded," I tell him. "We'll probably even find a parking spot after another lap or two around the entire perimeter here."

"The worst!" he shouts, but he's laughing.

Inside, the mall is a nightmare.

"How many presents do you have to buy?" Cam asks glumly.

"Actually, just one," I say. "For my mom."

"That's it?" Cam asks.

"Yeah." This makes me a little sad, but it's the truth. We're in the middle of a department store, and I look around somewhat helplessly. "What should I get her?"

Cam scans the store too. "I dunno," he says. "Which line's the shortest? Look, there's nobody over in shoes."

"I'm not buying her shoes."

We wander past a Christmas display.

"How about an ornament?" Cam says. But I can't imagine adding anything to the tree my mother and I already decorated. "Oh!" Cam grabs my arm. "Sulie! Duh!" He grabs an empty picture frame off a display and shoves it into my arms. "Let's go," he says.

"Wait, what? You want me to give her an empty picture frame?"

"I want you to fill it up for her."

I swallow and look down at the frame, and I know he's right. It's the perfect gift.

"Wait. Get two," he says, handing me another.

"Why?"

"Your secret boyfriend? Aren't you going to give him a present?"

"I don't have a boyfriend."

"OK. Well, get two anyway. Just in case. I'm not coming back here." Cam looks around at the swarms of shoppers in disgust and starts dragging me toward the register.

Cam's moms gave us a bunch of money before we left the house and insisted that I force Cam to eat lunch, so we make our way to the food court.

"I can't," Cam says, looking out over the teeming masses of diners. "Please don't make me."

"You have to eat," I say. "I promised."

"Not here," Cam says. "Anywhere but here."

We go to Tony Baloney's. We say a weird, "Hi, Grandma Nell," as we walk past Tony's flower boxes. Cam eats two pastrami sandwiches, chips, cole slaw, and both of our pickles, and I know both his moms will be thrilled.

"Thanks for dragging me out of bed this morning," he says. "I still kind of hate you for it, but I feel a little better."

"I hate to see you hurting," I say.

"I'm still freaking out," Cam says. "I mean, I have no idea what I'll be doing this time next year. That's crazy! How are you doing this, Sulie? Doesn't it just terrify you not to have a plan?"

I wipe my mouth carefully. "Actually," I say. "I do have a plan."

"Oh yeah?" I can tell he thinks I'm kidding. "Let's hear it."

"I got a job," I tell him. "Working with the homeless."

"What?"

"And I applied to UNC to study social work, maybe make a career out of helping people."

Cam is looking at me like he's never seen me before in his life.

I tell him about Brandi's mom dying and her bringing back the sunflower purse and about the mission and about Sarah and her new job in the school system.

"Why didn't I know this? Why didn't I know any of this?"

"Because I didn't tell you. I don't know why," I say. "I guess we've both been really busy. I'm sorry."

Cam looks really sad. "I think I should take some more days off," he says.

When I drop him off at home, both of his moms are obviously waiting. They throw the door open together, and I see him hug them both at once. They wave and smile at me as I drive away, and I know that, no matter what happens at the NYC cattle calls, Cam is going to be OK.

Chapter Twenty-Three

I head straight for home, knowing what I have to do to finish my Christmas gifts on time even though it kind of terrifies me to do it. I'm suddenly very aware of all the ugly drawings stuffed in the bottom of my sunflower purse. It's like they're all whispering that I can't do it. That bag has been getting heavier and heavier, and I'm tired of it. I slam on my brakes. I salvage my phone and my wallet but chuck the bag and its unpleasant contents on top of a neighbor's curbside trash pile. I drive faster the rest of the way down the street, my car a million pounds lighter.

I lock myself in my room with my sketchbook, and I don't come out until my mother tells me dinner's ready. I can't remember the last time we ate together, but it's Christmas Eve, and she's made a lasagna and set the table with her good plates. Instead of wine, we both drink sparkling cider out of her good stemware, and we talk about everything except the one person we're both thinking about the most and missing with all our hearts. It's tough, but we get through it.

On Christmas morning, I momentarily forget that Grandma's gone. I wake up to the smell of Sunday cakes and hurry out to the kitchen, but then I see my mom standing there in Grandma's apron, and the loss hits me again, hard. A huge lump in my throat doesn't want me to go on breathing. I swallow it down and force a smile. "You're baking."

"I'm not as good as you are." My mom frowns at a cooling rack full of lopsided, sunken cakes.

"Want some help?" I ask.

"I'd love that," she says.

I can't remember the last time my mom smiled at me like that. I let go of some of my sadness, and we put on some Christmas music and bake a fresh batch of Sunday cakes together.

"So, what time is this boyfriend of yours coming for dinner?" she asks me. "I'm making a ham, OK? I should have asked you—does he eat ham?"

I cringe. "I don't have a boyfriend anymore," I tell her. "It's just the two of us for dinner."

"What happened?" my mom asks.

I almost tell her, "Nothing," but instead I tell an edited-for-primetime version of what really happened. "We were hanging out when Cam got cut at his audition, and I just left Serge all by himself and went running off to comfort Cam. I think I really hurt his feelings."

"He sounds kind of insecure."

"Yeah," I say. "I guess he is."

"I'm sorry it didn't work out," she says.

"Me too."

We finish the cakes and frost them and eat a few for breakfast. "No calories on Christmas," my mother jokes. When we're done, she says, "Do you want to open your gift?"

We've never done huge piles of presents at Christmas. A weird fat man in red pants never once broke into our house while we slept and left behind a mountain of shiny new toys, and I've never minded. My mom always gives me one big gift, and it's always been enough. As we head toward the tree, I realize that this is the first year I won't have a gift from Grandma Nell under the tree too, some quirky, picked-up-on-one-of-her-excursions souvenir and a great story to go with it. But I think about how much she's given me since she passed away—the night of the blessing bags, a burgeoning friendship with Brandi, a job, a future, an unforgettable rendition of "The Dock of the Bay"—and I'm grateful.

"You go first," I tell my mom and hand her my present.

She covers her face and weeps when she opens it, and I think I've made a terrible mistake, but when she looks up at me, she's smiling through her tears.

"Oh, Sulie!" she says, reaching over the discarded gift wrap to hold me tight. "It's gorgeous! So beautiful! It's..." She lets go of me and looks back at the picture frame in her lap.

Inside is a drawing of Grandma Nell, not as she was at the end of her life, sickly and despondent, and not exactly how we both remember her either. It's an otherworldly image, her face as we knew it with a heavenly quality superimposed on it, some of her wrinkles smoothed out, an extra twinkle in her eyes. There's a tiny smudge in the corner where I cried on it while I worked, but I left it there because nothing in life is flawless. There is no such thing as perfection.

My mom runs her hand over Grandma's face. "You are so talented, my daughter," she says and looks up at me. "I love you so much."

I can't remember the last time my mother said that to me.

"I love you too," I say, but it's hard to get the words out.

When it's my turn, I open a big box with a map inside. "Thanks?" I say.

My mom smiles nervously. "It's a road trip," she says. "If you want to go. I thought we could take a few days together and maybe follow your grandmother's example. Get out and about a little. We can go anywhere you want. Pick a spot on the map."

"Wow," I say. "That's actually really great. I'd love to." I unfold the map. The whole United States is spread out in front of me.

"I have to admit, it's a little selfish." My mother twists her hands in her lap. "I was hoping we could maybe spread the last of your grandmother's ashes along the way?"

"I'd like that," I say.

"I figure we'll just see how it goes, and when we have, you know, our first significant mother-daughter moment together, we'll let the ashes fly right there, no matter where we are."

"I love it," I say. "And so would Grandma. That's the perfect plan."

My mom looks really happy. "We can leave whenever you want," she says. "You have a bunch of time off school right now, even." She looks kind of hopeful.

"OK," I say. "But I don't know about this week, because I said I'd go in to work, try to help them wrap some things up before the end of the year."

"Work?"

Oh, shit.

"Yeah," I say. "I kind of have a part-time job."

So, we sit underneath the Christmas tree and eat a couple more Sunday cakes, and I tell my mother everything about the blessing bags and Brandi and Sarah and Sarah's interview suit and her flushed cheeks. I tell her I thought it would be good to explore a degree in social work, and that I've applied to UNC for the fall, that I don't have many required courses left for graduation, and that I actually proactively emailed my guidance counselor about rearranging my schedule to accommodate early release so I can put in even more hours at the mission this coming semester.

"I didn't know any of this," she says. "I've been so wrapped up in myself that I haven't been paying you enough attention, and I'm sorry. I realized the other day when it turned out I had no idea who you were dating that I'm really out of touch. Now I find out you've gotten a job! I wish you'd felt like you could tell me about all of this as it was happening."

"I'm sorry too," I say. "I've been…weird for the past few weeks. I'm sorry for shutting you out. But I think this is what I want to do next year, and I'm telling you now."

"I'm glad you are."

"Me too. I mean, I want you to know what's going on. Who my boyfriend is and isn't, where I work. You should come down to the mission sometime and check it out."

My mother smiles, and I think she's going to hug me, but she jumps up and yells, "Oh my God!"

"What?"

"Did we just have a significant mother-daughter moment?"

I laugh, my mouth full of Sunday cake. "I think we did."

"I'm going to go get your grandmother."

We put coats on over our pajamas and run out to the front lawn where, as if some movie special-effects guy were on call, a few tiny little snow flurries have just begun to fall.

My mom holds her party bag out and runs across the lawn, and little bits of Grandma mingle with the snow as it sinks contentedly to Earth.

"This is perfect," my mom says. "I think all along, I just wanted her here." She's laughing and crying.

"Me too," I say, and I give her a real hug. As we head back into the house, I stop her. "Wait," I say. "You have an eyelash."

One of her dark lashes has settled on her cheek. I place it on the tip of my finger and tell her to close her eyes, make a wish, and blow. She does what I say. When she opens them, her eyelash is gone.

"My wish will come true!" she says, and I hope she's right. If she is, it won't be because she blew the lash into the swirling snow, though. As soon as she closed her eyes, I put it in my mouth and swallowed it.

Cam comes over midday, and we still haven't gotten dressed, but it doesn't matter because he's still in his pajamas too. He's thrown a jacket and the sloppy scarf I made him on over them. There's a little bit of snow in his hair, and his cheeks are red from the cold, and I try really hard not to think about how much I'm going to miss seeing him walk through my front door on a daily basis next year.

"I brought you a present," he says, and I open it right away. It's another map of the United States.

"Road trip?" I say. I can't believe this. Of all the gifts in all the world...

"No," he says. "I mean, well, yeah, maybe, if you want to. I hadn't thought of that." He takes the map from me and opens it. There are little dots and labels all over the place. "It's a map to your grandmother," he says. "The Senior Stars helped me with it. I got a whole bunch of them to tell me what they were doing with your grandmother's ashes, and they sent me tons of locations and stories to go with most of them too. Look." He points to the edge of the map where he's written, "Paris→." "She even made it to Europe!" he says.

"Thank you," I say, trying very hard not to cry. "This is amazing. I can't believe you found the time to do all of this."

"Like I said," he tells me, "the Stars helped a lot. They're such a cool bunch of ladies. Some of them are even on social media. Did you know?" He laughs. "They add a special kind of cray-cray to my news feed."

"Thank you," I say again. "I love this."

I kind of want him to go away now so I can be alone with the map, bawling my eyes out over every single story, but Cam's smelled Sunday cakes, so he plops down in the living room and helps himself to some of our leftovers. I sigh and put the map away for later. Maybe my mother and I can use it to plan part of our road trip. I grab my sketchbook, and I sit next to Cam and draw the side of his face and the way the lights from the Christmas tree play across it. He looks relaxed, happy, and very much alive. Nothing terrifying appears on the page.

I tell Cam that I saw a crochet circle on the Senior Stars schedule my grandma left behind and ask him whether he thinks his old-lady friends would let me come a few times, pick up some pointers. He tells me he thinks they absolutely would and that, in all honesty, I should go because as much as he loves the scarf I made him, my crochet skills need a lot of work, and he's sure he'll be needing all those sweaters I promised him next winter.

He says his moms dipped into their savings and did some last-minute shopping themselves. They added an airline gift certificate to his stocking so he can fly to New York as much as he needs to over the next few months—as many times as it takes to get a spot in a company. I tell him I'm really happy for him, and I actually mean it.

"Too bad the snow is stopping," he says as he stands up to leave. He's having an early dinner with his moms and his aunt and uncle and then going to visit Mia. "It would have been fun to build a snowman, wouldn't it?" He smiles as he slips his jacket on, lighting up our whole living room. "Remember when we—" He stops and looks at me, serious-faced. "Sorry," he says. "I keep doing that to you. I keep bringing her up."

"My grandma?" I nudge him. "It's OK." I take a deep breath. "Remember that huge snowman we made with Grandma Nell during that crazy storm in the fourth grade? The one that was as tall as she was?"

Cam smiles again. "Yeah," he says. "That was awesome."

"I miss her so much today," I tell him.

"I know," he says. I hug him, and he holds me Mom-Kelly tight.

Chapter Twenty-Four

My mom and I decide we can't stay in our pajamas for Christmas dinner, even if it's just the two of us. My mom puts on slacks and a red sparkly sweater I haven't seen her wear in a long time, and I put on my long black skirt and a scoop-neck top and wear one of Grandma Nell's narrowest scarves as a headband, tying it underneath my hair so I can feel it hanging down between my shoulder blades. I fasten a crystal-studded snowman brooch to the shoulder of my shirt, a little bit of Grandma's left-behind bling.

My mom and I make dinner together. There's the ham my mother mentioned earlier, but also sweet potatoes, homemade cranberry sauce, green bean casserole, and rolls. She's pulled out all the stops because she thought we were having company. I'm sorry if she's disappointed and some of the food might go to waste, but I'm glad we're making so many different dishes because it's going to feel like more of a holiday than if we'd just had a regular meal. There might even be a few more significant mother-daughter moments in our near future as we rub elbows in the kitchen.

I'm rinsing mixing bowls at the sink when I hear my mom talking to someone in the living room. When I go to see who it is, I almost faint right over into the Christmas tree at the sight of Serge handing my mom a laughably oversized poinsettia in a foil-covered pot.

"Serge?" I say.

"Hi." His face is blank, emotionless; he has a crap-ton of eye makeup on.

"Um, Mom? This is Serge."

"I know!" My mother looks positively delighted. "We just met. And he gave me this lovely plant! See?" She smiles at Serge and says, "Wait here. I have a present for you too."

My mom leaves with the poinsettia, and Serge and I just look at each other.

"I hope it's OK that I came," he says, but I don't have time to answer because my mother is already back and she's shoving a small, foil-wrapped gift into his hands.

Serge thanks her and opens it carefully. Instead of ripping the paper, he slides his finger under the flap at the end of the package and pulls the wrapping off so cleanly we could use it again if we wanted to. He holds his present up to his nose and gives it a sniff.

"It's cologne!" my mother exclaims in case Serge just arrived here from a planet without men's fragrances. "And it's named after a famous ballet dancer!"

"Thank you," he says. I can see by his face that he's extremely touched by the thought behind the gift and that he will never, ever, under any circumstances, use it.

"Why don't you two sit by the tree and chat while I finish getting dinner ready?" my mother says. She is positively gleeful.

I told her he wasn't my boyfriend anymore, right? I could have sworn I did.

Obediently, we go sit in the living room. My sketchbook is still open on the coffee table, and Serge frowns at the not-quite-finished drawing of Cam sitting in the exact spot he now occupies. He takes off his coat and pulls something from an inside pocket.

"I brought you something," he says. "I'm sorry I didn't wrap it."

He hands me the bubble mailer with his dance academy's return address on it. It's still unopened; he really never watched his brilliant performance.

"Thanks," I say.

"Nobody else would have asked to see it again," he says. "I never even have anybody in the audience. The way you got what I was saying with that piece, that connection we had, it really means something to me."

"Yeah," I say. "Well. That's what *friends* are for." I don't mean to sound bitter, but I can't help it. "Hang on," I tell him a little bit grudgingly. "I have something for you too."

Mine is wrapped, so I have to watch Serge go through his whole painstaking preserve-the-paper routine while I'm bursting to know what he thinks of the gift. I want to wrestle the thing away from him and tear it open, show him the right way to open a damned present.

"You drew me," he says. He's staring at a sketch of himself, just his head and shirtless shoulders, looking out through the glass of the picture frame Cam picked out for me at the mall. His eyes are dark and lined in black, his mouth is tense. His hair is standing up like it did the night of the Senior Showcase. The muscles in his neck are taut. He doesn't say it's good or anything like a normal, polite person would do. "Do I really look like this?" He just keeps staring at the picture.

"No," I say. "The drawing's not perfect. There's no such thing as perfection."

"Thank you, Sulie."

I expect him to put the picture aside, toss it on top of his coat, but he doesn't. He just keeps holding on to it.

My mom calls us to the dinner table, and we all sit down, but she's put Serge's grown-on-steroids poinsettia right in the middle of the table, and none of us can see each other. My mother laughs and moves the plant, but as soon as she does, I wish she'd put it back because Serge is sitting right across from me, staring at me hard.

Nobody says anything as we start to eat, and my mom says, "Maybe I should put some Christmas music on," filling some of the silence with low-volume carols. She asks Serge about his dancing, and he tells her about his scholarship in Utah. She says she's been to some of Cam's shows and maybe she's seen him before. "Were you in *The Nutcracker*?" she tries.

"Which one?" he asks. "We do it every year."

My mom has to think back over several years. "Hmmm," she says. "How about the one where Camden was a mouse?"

"I was a mouse that year too," he says.

"I remember you," she tells him, even though the mice all wear oversized mouse heads and nobody can ever see their faces. "You were really good."

"Thanks," Serge says, and I swear he finally cracks a small smile.

My mom and I clear the table, and Serge offers to help.

"Here," my mom tells him. "Set out these dessert plates."

The doorbell rings as I scrape and stack the dinner dishes. My mom's uncovering yet more Sunday cakes and has icing on her fingers. "Serge?" she says. "Can you see who that is for me?"

Serge disappears but doesn't come back with a visitor or a delivery or anything, so I wipe my hands on a kitchen towel and go look for him. He's holding the front door open, and a stunned-half-to-death Camden is staring at him, open-mouthed.

My mom's gotten curious too and comes up behind me. "Camden! Honey, come in. It's freezing out there."

Serge steps aside, and Cam finally crosses the threshold. "Thanks," he says. "Sorry." He looks at me, then my mom, then Serge. "I didn't know you had company."

"Nonsense," my mother says. "You know Serge, right? Have dessert with us. I'll go brew some coffee. Regular or decaf?"

"Regular," we all say at the same time, and she goes back into the kitchen.

Cam's clutching something to his chest. It's my sunflower bag.

"What are you doing with that?" I ask him.

"Oh, here." He hands it to me. "I was just out walking, and I found it on the side of the road. You're a total mess, you know that?"

"I threw it away!" I tell him. I laugh in a slightly maniacal way. "This is unbelievable! This bag just keeps coming back to me!" I chuck the bag on the floor and a bunch of crumpled paper falls out.

"What's all this?" Cam asks, stooping to pick it up.

"It's you," I tell him. "And you too." I look at Serge. "Come see," I say with a sigh.

We go into the living room, and I smooth each crumpled picture, lay them all out on the floor. My two closest friends in the world are lying there in various states of agony right beneath my Christmas tree. Grandma's there too, sick and wasted. I can taste my dinner again in the back of my throat.

"Whoa," Cam says.

Serge bites his lip and frowns at the drawings.

"I wanted to get rid of them," I say. "I just wanted to get rid of all the bad stuff."

"We should do something with these," Cam says.

"We could eat them," I say. I might even sound a little hopeful.

Only Serge knows I'm not kidding. Cam laughs.

We all stare at the imperfect, crumpled pictures.

"I have. The best. Idea!" Cam is suddenly smiling more brightly than all of our Christmas lights put together.

I ask my mom if we can hold off on dessert for a while, and she sounds puzzled but says it's no problem. The three of us put on our coats and tell her we're going for a walk. Serge's face is stuck halfway between bewildered and bemused, but he doesn't question Cam and follows us out the front door into the cold.

"I'm not sure I understand," Serge says as we head down my street in the dark. "When you say we'll give all this stuff to Grandma Nell…how's that going to work, exactly?"

"See, there's this duck pond," Cam starts. Then he stops himself. "Sulie, you tell him."

"There's this duck pond," I say, "where Grandma used to take us when we were little."

"Tell him about that time I fell in." Cam laughs hard.

"That has nothing to do with this." Sometimes Cam exasperates me. He really does.

"But it's funny." He laughs some more.

"Whatever. So, this one time, Cam fell in and got filthy. OK?"

"It's a better story when I tell it the right way, but OK. Go on."

Serge is looking at both of us like we're crazy.

"Anyway, this duck pond? It's where Cam chose to put his part of Grandma's ashes."

"Ah," Serge says.

"Wait." Cam stops walking, so we stop too. "You know about the ashes?" He looks at Serge in disbelief.

"Yeah."

Cam shakes his head. "OK," he says, and we all start walking again.

"So, the duck pond is a place where you feel connected to your grandmother?" Serge asks me.

"Yeah," I say. "Cam's right. We should chuck all the bad stuff in there, and she'll take care of it for us."

Serge nods as if this makes sense, even though I'm well aware that it doesn't.

"I think I get why she did this now," Cam says. "Grandma Nell? I think I get why she wanted her ashes all over the place."

"Me too," I say. "It's like she wanted to be anywhere we might need her or want to feel close to her, like she wanted to be able to watch over all of us at once."

"You're really lucky," Serge says, and even though it sounds rude to say someone's lucky that their grandmother died, I know exactly what he means.

The walk to the park is longer than it used to seem when we were kids, and we're all freezing by the time we get there. I pull the flattened pictures out of my purse. "So, do I just, like, chuck 'em in?" I ask.

"Wait," Cam says. He scrounges around on the ground and finds a handful of stones. He puts a few inside the first picture, an image of my grandmother's unhappy, emaciated face, and wraps the paper around them. "Go for it," he says as he hands the strange little package back to me. "Let 'er fly."

I pull my arm back and throw the ball of paper and rocks as hard as I can. I let out a cry of frustration and anger as I do it. The bad stuff lands right in the middle of the duck pond and sinks. I'm breathing heavily as I watch the ripples where it broke the surface slowly disappear.

"Wow," I say. "That felt amazing!"

"Do it again." Cam hands me some more rocks.

"I hate cancer!" I scream as I throw another drawing of my sick grandmother into the water.

"Here."

I'm crying a little bit now, but Cam hands me more rocks, and I use them to make another paper ball.

"I hate when people leave!" I shout. That one makes a splash as it lands, and I laugh a little. "This is awesome," I say, sniffling and smiling in spite of my watery eyes. "You want to try?" I look back and forth between my friends.

"Sure," Cam says. "You got a pencil?"

"Do *I* have a *pencil*?"

Cam laughs. I dig in the sunflower bag and come up with the dull stub of one of my drawing pencils, a 2B. Cam takes it and turns over one of the pictures. "I…didn't…make…Queen…

City," he says slowly as he writes. He wraps his bad stuff up in some rocks and screams deep from the gut as he chucks it almost clear across the pond. "You're right," he says afterward, smiling and a little breathless. "That does feel good. Serge, do one."

Serge looks uncertain.

"Here," I tell him. I pass him the pencil and a picture of his own broken face. He turns it over and writes on it.

"I hate my mother," he says and pitches his crumpled paper like a baseball into the pond.

"See?" I say. "That's good, right?"

Serge nods vigorously but doesn't speak.

Cam takes another picture. "I'm...scared...about...next... year! Ahhhhhhhhrrrrrrrrrrrrrg!"

"My turn," I say. "I hate being lonely!" I scream into the night.

Serge writes carefully on the back of another picture. "I'm afraid to feel anything," he says sadly and chucks it into the pond.

"There's one left," I say. "And I think I'm good."

"Me too," Cam says. "Take it, Serge. It's a picture of you."

Serge thinks for a long time before he writes on the back of his tortured image. A cold wind blows around us and we all shiver.

"I broke up with Sulie," he finally says morosely and hurls it into the pond. We all watch it sink in silence.

"I thought you said he wasn't your boyfriend," Cam says, looking at me sideways with a smug little smile on his face.

"You heard him," I say. "He's not."

"Yes, I am," Serge says, still looking out over the pond. "At least, I want to be."

We're all quiet and cold a little longer. Serge and I finally catch each other's eyes and smile just a little. Cam sighs and rolls his eyes at both of us.

"Let's go home," I say.

We start to walk back to my house. Serge reaches for my hand, and I let him take it and give him a little squeeze. Even though my cold hand would be much better off in my pocket, I don't let go. We walk close together so our shoulders are touching.

Cam looks at us and shakes his head. "When were either of you going to tell me about this?" he says. Neither of us answers him, and he sighs and shakes his head some more, and we walk in silence for a block or two, heads bowed against the cold. "Hey," Cam says. "Sulie. You never told me what you did with your part of the ashes."

I can feel Serge's laser-focused eyes on me.

"Sulie? What did you do with your piece of Grandma Nell?"

I take a deep breath. "I don't want to tell you," I say. "OK? I love you to death, but there are just some things I can't talk about with you."

"Fair enough," Cam says, nodding. I'm afraid he's going to be mad, but he smiles. "I love you to death too," he says. "And Serge? I like you pretty good too."

Serge laughs. "This is a really weird night," he says. "Right? Or is this just normal for you guys?"

Cam and I both laugh, but neither of us is quite sure how to answer him.

"Come to think of it," I say. "This is kind of a weird night. How did you find my purse anyway? Cam? Why were you out wandering around our neighborhood in the dark on Christmas Day?"

"Oh," he says. "I was just…sad, I guess. Needed to think."

"About the audition?" Serge asks. "That's a tough break, man. But it's their loss."

"I guess it has to do with that," Cam says. "I went to give Mia her Christmas present, and she broke up with me."

"What?" I'm shocked. Elated, thrilled, over the moon. And seriously jaw-hitting-floor dumbfounded.

"Yeah." Cam sighs. "She said she couldn't really see a future with me."

"Just because you're not going to dance with Queen City? What a bitch!" Serge says.

I sigh. Damn it. "Wait a minute," I say. "Was this before or after you gave her your present?"

"After," he says. "Right after."

"Harsh!" Serge shakes his head.

"What, if I may be bold enough to ask, was the present?" I say.

"Candy." Cam looks puzzled. "I gave her candy."

"Mia doesn't eat," Serge points out.

"She doesn't?" Cam furrows his brow.

"I don't think so," I tell him.

"Really?" Cam looks shocked.

"Really," Serge says, and I nod.

"But it's not just that," I say. "There's definitely more to this. What kind of candy was it, Cam?"

"I dunno? Peppermints, I guess? A ton of 'em. But they were in this super awesome reindeer dispenser thing?" He laughs. "It's hysterical, really. It's like this huge stuffed reindeer and, when you push down on his antlers, he craps the candies out!"

"You gave her a pooping reindeer for Christmas?" I ask him.

"No!" he says. "Well, yes, but it's not as bad as you make it sound. It had a little bow on it and everything. Honestly, Su-Su, it was cute! And so, so funny. You would have laughed your ass off."

"Yeah," I say. "But I'm not your girlfriend. I'm not Mia Nardone."

"Shit," Cam says as we get back to my house. "Do you really think that was it? I mean, I was just trying not to get her anything too…you know…romantic or personal or whatever."

"Well, congratulations," I tell him. "You didn't. No wonder she can't see a future with you."

"Really?"

"Really! Cam! Right now, after hearing that story? I don't even know if *I* can see a future with you."

"Me either," Serge says. "For real." He's smiling, trying not to laugh.

"What do I do?" Cam looks a little desperate.

"We'll fix it," I say. "We'll go to the mall tomorrow." I squeeze Serge's hand. "All three of us. We'll go pick her out a necklace that has 'future' written all over it. If that's what you really want."

"Thanks," he says. "I'll think about it."

When we get inside, my mom seems really happy that we're back. "I'm so glad your friends are here," she tells me.

"One friend," I say. Then Serge and I share a secret smile. "And one boyfriend."

My mom looks back and forth between Cam and Serge for a second.

"Serge," I say, annoyed. "Serge, Mom. Serge is the boyfriend."

"I know," she says. "I knew that!"

Serge looks confused, and Cam tries really hard to hide his laughter. "Sunday cakes!" he says as we sit down to dessert. "These just never get old!"

"We've already eaten, like, a million of these today," I say, but I shove another one in my mouth anyway.

It's Serge's first time tasting them, and he looks a little uncertain.

"Sulie helped me bake these in honor of her grandmother," my mom tells him, and his head snaps up so he can stare at me. I kind of want to reassure him, and I kind of think it would be funny not to too.

I decide to take the high road and let him know it's OK to eat. "It's a pretty standard cake recipe," I tell him, code for "There are no dead people in these."

He takes a bite and smiles, tells us both how good they are, just like a normal, polite person would do. It's just one of the many Christmas miracles I've gotten to experience tonight.

When Serge says he should get going, Cam says that he has to go too. My mother tries to foist a bunch of leftovers on them both, but Cam says his moms are drowning in leftovers. Serge seems really grateful, though. Cam and I both walk him to his car and stand there while he puts the food and his gifts inside.

"Listen, I'm sorry if I crashed your date tonight," Cam says, but he doesn't look very sorry. He's grinning like a big goofball, warming up the cold December night. "See, though? This is what happens if my friends don't tell me that they're dating."

"Noted," I say. I'm trying to use telepathy to tell him to go away so I can be alone with Serge, but he just keeps standing there.

"Hey," he says to Serge. "No ballet this week. We should get everyone together. Hang out."

"Actually," Serge says. "James wants to have a New Year's Eve party. Some kind of themed thing. Turns out I kind of owe him a favor." Serge grimaces at the memory of their last party. "So I said we could use my place. Obviously, you're invited."

"Wow," Cam says. "That sounds awesome. I promise not to wreck the joint again. Man, I can't believe your mom wasn't so pissed about that coffee table that she banned us all for life."

"Well," Serge says. He sighs into the cold air, and some sadness leaves his body in a little white cloud. "She doesn't know about it. It's complicated. Maybe I can tell you about it tomorrow if we go shopping or whatever."

"OK," Cam says. "Sounds good." He still doesn't make a move to leave the driveway.

"Can you go now?" I finally ask him. "I'm freezing my ass off, and I want to talk to Serge before he leaves."

Cam laughs. "I think it's your subtlety I love about you the most, Su-Su," he says, and wrestles me into a hug. He hugs Serge too, and then finally takes off toward home at a jog.

"I thought he'd never leave," I tell Serge, but he just shakes his head and smiles.

"Actually, I'm really glad we all got to hang out together," he says. "I've been...jealous of him. Since before I got to know you, even, you know? Because of how hard he works at ballet and the way everyone always likes him. And since we started seeing each other, I've been afraid of losing you to him. But I get it now. And I'm sorry."

"I think you're entitled to a few trust and abandonment issues," I tell him. "I've got plenty of those myself."

Serge laughs just a little. "We're a mess," he says.

"I'm OK with messes," I tell him, and I put my arms around him and kiss him until we both almost freeze to death, gulping down as much of him as I can before he drives away.

Chapter Twenty-Five

This party feels a lot like the last one, but it's different too. For one thing, there's a lot more space for dancing since Serge never replaced his coffee table, and that's good because there are a few more dancers this time. Also, there's a theme tonight: Prohibition. Which is hysterical, because almost everyone is already pretty drunk. We're all dressed as flappers and gangsters, and there won't be any *Dirty Dancing* tonight because James's playlist is all twenties stuff: big band, swing, jazz. The dance kids are all doing the Charleston (which, if you ask me, doesn't look much unlike the knees and elbows dance they all did last time) and the Lindy Hop. I'm trying really hard not to be nervous as I watch them jump around and swing each other through the air.

Mia looks absolutely gorgeous tonight, wearing a black fringy flapper dress, a new silver necklace that has *future* written all over it, and a zoot-suited Cam wrapped around her little finger. James has brought a date who doesn't seem like much of a dancer, but he does seem like a really good sport, bopping around in time to the music, wearing a pinstriped vest and pants. He introduces himself as Tate and says he's hoping to go to law school. He and James can't seem to take their eyes off each other, and I'm happy for James; I really am.

Natalie's brought two dates, twin lacrosse players from her school. That's how she introduces them to everyone. "They're twins. They play lacrosse." I never do get the guys' names, but I tell them to help themselves to a drink from Serge's bar, which they do. Often. They're obviously not that into dancing, either, but they both seem really into Natalie. She's wearing a super-short red flapper dress covered in beads and sequins. I feel positively plain in comparison, even though the other girls have assured me my outfit is "cute." I've recycled my black funeral dress and "pumps," adding a sequined headband, a vintage crystal-encrusted brooch from Grandma's collection, and a black feathered boa for the occasion. The cheap boa is shedding feathers like crazy; tomorrow it will look like a flock of crows migrated through Serge's glass house overnight.

None of these people will be together next year. Some of them will probably never even see each other again after they graduate. James is moving to Florida to dance with a ballet company there, Mia's hoping to get into the Boston Conservatory, and Natalie's quitting ballet to pursue an acting career in California, which I think means she's probably going to wind up as a stripper. They're all going to leave this place and each other, and they're all dancing anyway, like they don't have a care in the world.

"Here," Serge says, handing me a drink. He glances at a TV on mute in the corner. "Not long until midnight," he says. "Cheers."

He looks incredible in a dark suit and a fedora pulled low over his eyes. He's not wearing any eye makeup at all, and there's a softness, a sweetness, in his gaze as he looks at me that makes me feel half-drunk already.

I take a sip of my cocktail. It's as bad as his smoothie. "What is this?" I ask him.

"James says it's a Southside," he tells me. "Al Capone supposedly drank them."

I take another careful sip. Then another. Maybe after a few more drinks, it won't bother me either that everybody leaves. Maybe if I drink enough Southsides, I'll jump into the fray and join the Charleston.

Just kidding.

"How was dinner with your mom?" Serge asks me. My mom and I went to a restaurant together before she took off for a party of her own with some of her support-group friends, none of whom, I'm guessing, are dancing the Charleston right now.

"It was good," I say. "We spent most of it talking about our spring break road trip."

"You know where you're headed yet?"

"We've got more than ten spots we want to hit," I say. "We're working off the map that Cam made. We're going to go visit at least ten of my grandmother's final resting places. And we're adding in a few stops of our own along the way too. You know, for some extra bonding time or whatever."

"Sounds good."

If he's bitter or jealous of my plans with my mother and all the significant mother-daughter moments we've managed to squeeze in over the holidays, it doesn't show. And he'll be busy himself over spring break, flying to Utah to check out his new campus. I hear it's still cold out there well into the springtime, so I'm working on a new scarf and hat for him to take. I think I'm getting a little better at crocheting, but the hat's looking a little funky. I'm thinking of crocheting some pieces to hand out at the mission as well—I plan to be working there a lot more in the new year, and I think its clients would benefit from the warmth of some handmade-just-for-them scarves and shawls. I'm sure I must be mistaken, but Cam seems kind of relieved not to be the sole focus of my crochet efforts anymore.

Serge puts his arm around me and pulls me close. "I don't know if I can wait until the ball drops to take you upstairs," he whispers.

"Who says you have to?" I ask him. I'm sleeping over. We all are. Serge wanted some company, and now he's got loads. "I bet nobody'd miss us."

I look around at all the crazy dancers filling up Serge's glass living room and see that every one of them is lost in his or her own world, alone in the middle of the crowd.

"Let's go," Serge says.

His bedroom is still oddly bare, but now he has the framed sketch I gave him standing on his desk, his one and only piece of décor. I pull him down onto his neatly made bed. Black feathers from my boa fly everywhere, and I laugh.

I hear everyone start counting downstairs, and I know that what's left of the year can be measured in mere seconds now, but I have no desire to run down and rejoin the party. Maybe it's the Southside at work in my brain, but I can't think of a better way to spend the last few seconds of this sea-change year than devouring as much as I can of Serge.

About the Author

A.L. Glennon has a Master of Arts degree from the Communication, Culture, and Technology Program at Georgetown University. She currently lives with her family in North Carolina, where she teaches high school English. She is the author of the YA novel *Wait for It*.

IngramElliott Publishing

IngramElliott is an award-winning independent publisher with a mission to bring great stories to light in print and on-screen. We publish stories with a unique voice that will translate well into film and television. Visit us at www.ingramelliott.com for more information.

Our *IngramElliott* imprint features full-length fiction and non-fiction titles designed with the book lover in mind.

Our *IE Snaps!* imprint features novella-length fiction in popular genres that are designed for a quick read on the go.

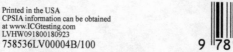